The Power Ball Murders

BENJAMIN MOORE

FIRST GARTH HENDERSON THRILLER WRITTEN BY BENJAMIN MOORE

Private Investigator Garth Henderson, a former NYPD vice squad and homicide detective, is up to his neck on a case involving a murdered Powerball lottery winner, who happens to be the wife of a prominent senator. His New York rip-and-run glory days on the task force have not prepared him for the hell he is about to go through solving this crime. Will he even make it out alive?

Table of Contents

PREFACE

Just to put your minds at ease, this is not a serial killer novel. There is no monster at the end with bleeding fangs, sporting clown make-up, living under the stairs. There is no "It puts the lotion in the basket' twisted, psychotic loner living in a dungeon. This book is more on the lines of a political thriller. A vendetta, revenge tale of sorts that included collateral damage. It was a political year, 2004 when I decided to turn this idea of a lottery winner getting killed into a book. The PowerBall Murders started off as a screenplay. My premier profession is as a writer for TV and film. This would be the first time I decided to turn one of my screenplays into a book at the behest of a good friend of mine, who had read the script. He uttered five words to me, after reading it... "Turn this into a book". I took Stephen Greenidge's advice. Usually it's the other way around, where a book gets adapted to a script and sells to a studio or network to get made. During the transition, my plot stayed the same... Private investigator, Garth Henderson tries to find out who killed the Senators wife, Jacqueline Caldwell a few days after she won the big ticket. All accounts pointed to a likely suspect, the husband. But it wasn't going to be that easy for the P.I. to solve this case. In the investigation, a rabbit hole had formed, that spanned multiple states and garnered multiple suspects. This murder became a conspiracy. I was a big fan of Dashiell Hammett, 'Maltese Falcon', Walter Mosley and James Patterson novels. Those *find me, catch me if you can,* premises were always fun to read. The detail that went into the killer's mind, where the chaser had to dive into the mindset of the chased, almost driving them insane and costing them their life in the interim. However, it was very necessary to catch a murderer. The audience for this type of book, has to be a lover of these type of murder mysteries. You root for the good guy to catch the bad guy, but hoping the killer(s) gives the cops a good run. I try to epitomize that chase in this novel, hoping the reader gets to follow along, eventually figuring it out around the same time the lead character does. This was a cynical murder that required some deep detecting on Whodunit and why. So, enjoy the journey.

Benjamin Moore.

CHAPTER 1

Sandy Lauson makes a beautiful corpse as I focus my Nikon on her prone form and snap a photo. *Coming from the robbery-homicide division* of Brooklyn, I didn't think being a private eye in Virginia would be so difficult. I mean, it's Virginia for goodness sakes, a commonwealth state that has a political community that prides itself on making its own laws. But Central Point, Caroline County, Virginia is also the birthplace of the Virginia Racial Integrity Act of 1924, which criminalized marriages between white and nonwhite persons. Back in 1967, a black and white couple named Richard and Mildred Loving decided to go off to Washington, D.C., and get hitched away from the eyes and ears of the Southern government. Later on, when they returned home to their tiny town of Caroline County, they were arrested by the county sheriff, who had received an anonymous tip. The Lovings were both charged under Virginia's anti-miscegenation law with "cohabiting as man and wife against the peace and dignity of the Commonwealth." Go figure. But I'm sure things have changed since then.

My only previous experience with the *Virginia is for Lovers* state was when I was a child and my family visited amusement parks like

Busch Gardens and Kings Dominion for summer entertainment. The view during the six or seven-hour drive was incredible. The colorful leaves in early autumn were breathtaking. I remembered it as a beautiful, peaceful place. So when I retired from the New York Police Department, I decided to move here for a slower pace.

There's nothing peaceful or beautiful about the scene before me now. I take another picture with my Nikon D700 camera and glance at the three-inch viewing monitor. Good shot.

"Sandy, turn over on your left side," I calmly tell her. Sandy does as I say. Blood oozes from her mouth and nose, slowly trickling on the ground. One of her Nine West shoes rests inches from her feet. A lace stocking is torn from her thigh to her ankle. "Wipe your tears, Sandy, you're ruining the makeup," I yell out again.

Sandy pulls out a tissue and dabs it softly around her eyes and nose. "This bastard is gonna pay for this, Garth. You hear me? He's going to pay for this with his life," she cries.

Not wanting to provoke an already emotional woman any further, I don't respond. I take another picture from an alternate angle. "Just a few more shots, Sandy. Slightly open your mouth just a little," I say.

Sandy doesn't say a word. She slowly parts her lips as tears stream down both sides of her face. I shake my head at the ruining of my half-assed makeup job. I am doing this hit-for-hire bust on some poor woman whose husband wanted her dead. They were going through a bitter divorce, and he was losing. It was a tumultuous ordeal with one young child caught in the middle. Alimony and child support were north of seven grand a month, and the guy was probably dishing out another two grand each month on hookers and prostitutes since his wife closed up shop on him. Ironically, he paid me $10,000 for the hit. *The nerve of him*, I thought as I took half of the money as down payment.

I remember like it was yesterday. I was sitting at the bar downing a Bud Light when a tall, dark man walked into Katy's and slipped me a note. It simply read, '*Quick cash for one day's work.*'

I slowly turned to the tall man and offered one simple reply: "Who I gotta kill?"

I was undercover on a stakeout, keeping an eye out for a group of trailer-trash meth addicts and crank dealers who were making violent rounds in the local bars. I guess my disguise of dirty jeans, torn T-shirt, and faded leather jacket gave him the wrong impression. I hadn't told him I was a killer-for-hire; he just assumed it.

My reply was followed by another note slipped to me. Inside was a picture of a woman and an address. Sandy. Oh, beautiful Sandy. In the photo she appeared as a timid, gorgeous woman with a curvy figure. I could see why her husband fell for her. But what would make a man want to go so far as to want her dead? It bothered me. Here, even in Caroline County, Virginia, the evil reeks.

I took the job. He never uttered a word while we hashed out the details on our first meeting. Just notes being passed like you would to a teller during a bank robbery. "Quiet or noisy?" I asked the tall man.

'*Just dead,*' his reply note read. I shook my head.

"Timetable?" I grunted to the silent man.

Still not a word, just another note. 'March 19th.' Why he picked that date I couldn't tell you, but he seemed stern and very locked in on his wishes.

'*Ten grand,*' the next note read.

"Meet back here next week with half down payment," I told him.

The tall man got up, but not before downing the last bit of his Johnnie Walker Black. Uttered one word, finally: "Hired." Then, just like that, he walked away. I looked around the room to see if anyone even noticed the mystery man leaving. He had a slow, easy, stealth-like walk, like he was gliding with the wind. He blended in with the darkly lit bar atmosphere like a ghost. No one even looked up when the door closed behind him.

So here I am, a hit man hired to kill a mother of one. Sandy gets up, dusts herself off, and somberly approaches me. "Can I see them?" she whispers.

I scroll through my Nikon viewfinder, showing her pictures of herself. "You look good dead," I say with a chuckle, trying to take her mind off the reality of this situation. Sandy doesn't even crack a smirk. I can sense a change in the timid woman I once met in a playground with her son on a seesaw. This ordeal has scarred her.

She slowly blinks and strolls over to the passenger side of my Buick Enclave. Sandy sits in the passenger seat and stares straight ahead into nothingness. Not every day you find out that the man you once loved and shared a bed with wants you dead. I understood her stoic demeanor. Nothing hurts more than when a friend has turned into an enemy.

I pack up my props from the staged murder scene. It had looked perfect. I'd used a few blood dye packs and packets of tomato sauce, and also some bullet shells scattered around as evidence of a shooting.

I'd even had some rope laced with drips of fake blood, just to show I had his wife tied up in the trunk. Then I had splattered whatever liquids I had lingering around to make a further mess of things. As I put everything away, I take another look back at the passenger seat of my car to see if Sandy has loosened up a little. She hasn't. A blank stare graces her face like someone who's just been told she has terminal cancer. It's unbelievable that a one-time Ms. Rhode Island beauty pageant winner and neighborhood *it* girl could come to this. This is the first time I've been concerned about her mental state, but I have a feeling it won't be my last.

CHAPTER 2

WE TAKE A DRIVE TO MY LITTLE office that's located on Cricket Lane in downtown Caroline County. It's a small-town neighborhood with a row of old storefronts that locals go to for bread, milk, and newspapers. They even have a little saloon and barbershop on the corner with one of those red, white, and blue twirls on the corner brick wall. This is as far away from my old New York City nightlife that you can get. My office is filled with private eye novels, decrepit furniture, and dusty lampshades. You would think this is a scene out of *The Maltese Falcon* and I am Humphrey Bogart's character, *Sam Spade*. I've even gone as far as getting a Stetson hat and a long trench coat. "You gotta look the part," my dad would always tell me. He should've known. He used to be a numbers runner and a booze smuggler who always kept himself sharp and focused.

Sandy does a once over, scanning the room before uttering her first words in sixty minutes. "Do you have a bathroom?" she whispers.

I look to the left and point to a door that reads *Bathroom*. She gives me a broken smile as best as she can to be courteous. She walks in and turns on the water. I go to my desk and start wrestling through some papers. I keep an ear open for the water to stop running just to prepare myself for dealing with such a broken woman.

Suddenly, right in front of me, her voice, just as clear as ever, blurts out, "So what now?"

Shocked, I look up and close my desk draw. "We show your husband—"

Abruptly, she cuts me off. "Ex-husband, damn it, ex-husband!" she yells.

"Excuse me, Ms. Lauson. As I was saying, we show your ex-husband the pictures at the precinct. The real graphic ones, just to mess with his head. Then we break the bad news to him."

Sandy slowly blinks, almost as if she doesn't think it will be that simple. "What bad news?" she says.

"That you're not actually dead," I tell her.

She folds her arms and paces in a circle, angry at how easy this is going to go down. Then she says, "I want to be there."

I shake my head in disagreement. "Ms. Lauson, I think its best that you don't. Just go home to your beautiful son and prepare for life without this man."

"No!" she says with even more tenacity. "I want to look the bastard who wanted me dead in the eyes."

Once again, knowing how these things can turn for the worse, I plead with her to change her mind. After about ten minutes of me trying to convince Sandy that the mere sight of this man at this moment can cause things to go very bad for a trial, she finally agrees. She grabs her coat off my sofa and furiously leaves. I close the door behind her, hoping for the best.

Not a minute goes by before I hear a knock. Thinking it's Sandy, I hesitantly mumble, "Come in." I look up to see the shadowy figure of a tall man standing in the doorway. At first glance I think it's the husband, Richard Lauson. *What nerve he has to show up here*, I think.

I take no chances as I slide my hand to my desk drawer, where my thirty-eight revolver sits, just in case I have to draw down on him. Then I look even harder at the man as flashes of Sam Spade and Humphrey Bogart pop into my head.

This figure's presence carries some power with it. His wingtip shoes echo as he moves closer to my desk. The floor creaks with every step as this heavy man with an erect stance walks toward me with his hands in his trench coat pockets. There is a confidence the shadowy figure exudes, like a mob boss entering a back room for a sit-down.

Then the figure steps one more time and crosses into the light. I do a double take before slightly sliding my chair back.

"Senator Caldwell?" I blurt out, surprised.

"Are you Garth Henderson?" he casually says.

"In the flesh," I joke back.

He slides an envelope onto my desk and glares at me. "My wife has been murdered, and I need you to find her killers," he resolutely says.

I look at the envelope and spin it around upright. There are two names written on it: Jacqueline Caldwell, his wife, and Senator Brandon Caldwell. This was a high profile murder I am very familiar with. It always spooked me.

"The woman I saw in the hallway looked pretty distraught. Is she going be all right?" he inquires. Wow, a politician that actually cares.

"Not for a while, Senator Caldwell," I toot back.

We look at each other for a moment, neither of us saying anything, and when I realize he's waiting for me to make the next move, I say, "I'm sorry to hear about your wife. But I'm curious, sir. You said killers, as in plural?"

The senator takes a deep breath. "Yes, I did. Is that going be a problem?" he throws back at me.

"Not at all, sir. Just curious how you can be so sure it was more than one killer."

The senator pulls out a clipping from the *Virginia Daily*. I can see that he did his homework and came fully prepared to sell me on this case. He throws the paper on the desk with a flick of his wrist. The headline reads in bold print: *Powerball winner hits for $110 million; remains anonymous.* I have to read it twice because I never knew anyone who hit the lotto that huge, not even a friend of a friend. Sure there have been a few thousand-dollar hits here and there, but $110 million is almost unbelievable.

I look up at the senator in disbelief. "Your wife hit Powerball for a hundred and ten million?" I gasp.

Before I can get another word out, he runs down what he knows as if he was on the investigation team himself. "Jacqueline was on her way from claiming her first installment when a late model burgundy four-door sedan ran her over. Just killed my wife like she was a dog off a leash".

Surprised at the level of detail, I glare at him like he's a suspect confessing to a murder. The kind of confession you see on that TV show, *The First 48*, when the suspect is tap dancing around the evidence while still wearing a bloody pair of shoes. The senator reads me well. My countenance displays a suspicion that's a dead giveaway.

"Now, you wanna consider me a suspect, go ahead. But don't waste too much of my time and money investigating me," he says, and he throws another envelope on the desk. This one has a bulge to it, the kind of bulge that has $10,000 written all over it. "Here's some start-up money. Just call me when you need more." And just like that, the senator walks out.

Subconsciously, I've had my hand on my desk drawer with my thirty-eight inside the whole time. His presence must've made me nervous.

CHAPTER 3

I take a drive over to the Tenth Precinct to close out this hit-for-hire case. I can't help thinking about how distraught Sandy was when she left my office. Though she wanted to be there when we bust her dirtbag husband, I vigorously convinced her not to come. Deep down inside, though, I kind of want her to be there to get some sort of redemption from her ordeal. Seeing us put the cuffs on him might ease her pain, but it's the right thing to do to let it be. I walk into the precinct located in the middle of town next to a lake. A few cops start humming the tune to Peter Falk's *Colombo* as soon as I step through the lobby doors. I raise my hand and wave hello to all of them as I make my way to the back. I arrive at private interrogation room number one and look through the window in the door. Two FBI agents are in conference with three police officers, and with them is Richard Lauson, the sobbing husband of Sandy Lauson. He's filed his missing persons report and given a bogus story about how he got a phone call, heard a scream, and the phone went dead. The cops bring in the pictures I took of his wife to show him. I lean against the wall as I continue to look in, waiting for the three famous words a guilty person yells when confronted with his act of violence: "Oh God, nooooo!" Right on cue, Richard screams out. He does a flip-flop on the floor. Even kisses the photos a few times to really piss everyone off. "Why, baby, whhyyyyy?" he continues. An agent grabs the pictures out of his hand. "Is this your wife, sir?" the agent calmly asks. Mr. Lauson nods his head up and down and trembles as he clinches his fists. By now his eyes have swelled puffy and mucus is running down his nose. Either he's had a change of heart and he regrets having his wife killed, or he's that good of an actor. I decide he's that good of an actor. After a few minutes, I've seen enough of the fake sorrow to the point of making me want to puke. I tap on the window to let the agents know the game is up then I walk in. Mr. Lauson spooks like he's seen a ghost, and catches his breath. His skin goes full pale as he turns his head to avoid eye contact with me. I walk right up to him, stoop down, grab the top his head, and turn it to where we are face-to-face. "Hi, Richard, remember me?" I smile. Richard just glares up at me with disdain in his faint blue eyes and spits on the floor. Immediately, a federal agent goes behind him and slaps the cuffs on him. Suddenly, I feel a brush against my shoulder followed by a blood-curdling, howling scream. *Oh no*, I think to myself. *Sandy*. Sandy Lauson has made it to the precinct and right into interview room number one. She screams and swings as hard as she can and slaps her ex-husband in the face. *Pow!* "I hate you!" she screams. Sandy spits in his face.

A shocked Richard looks at her almost with a sense of relief. "Baby, you're alive," he mutters with a slight smile. Then his smile turns into a frown as he quickly realizes the trouble he's in. Sandy continues ranting, tenaciously spewing all sorts of obscenities at Richard. The federal agent starts hustling Richard out of the back door while I take Sandy out the front. The whole thing is a huge mess.

I walk out into the precinct floor from the interrogation room and hear a few choice heckles thrown my way from the officers: "Nice work, Garth." "Good going, Perry Mason."

As I walk past one of the officer's desk, I see him fiddling with a lottery ticket. "What's that?" I curiously ask.

"Powerball ticket. Hundred thirty-three million this week," the officer, Detective Fuller, gloats. I walk closer to his desk and pick up the ticket and stare at it. I need to see more considering I am going to be knee deep in this Powerball thing. The senator's wife hit this Powerball for $110 million alone, and I want to know how it happened. It's pretty basic. A simple game of shading numbers in a box or having the computer do it for you, that's all. I turn to Sandy as she stands idle, waiting for me. "I'll be there in one minute, Sandy," I tell her.

Fuller grabs back his ticket. "Didn't take you for a gambling man, Garth," he says.

I grab the ticket back. "I'm not, just following up on a case I'm on. You ever hit?" I inquire.

Fuller grabs the ticket back again. "Once in ninety-eight, hundred fifty-five thousand," he replies. "Bought a pickup. Paid off my three-bedroom house. Partied and drank the rest away with my college buddies."

Still not satisfied with my ignorance of the game, I push for more information. "When is the winner announced?" I ask while snatching the ticket once more.

Fuller snatches his ticket back yet again and this time throws it in his desk drawer. "Every Saturday and Wednesday at eleven p.m. Winning numbers are announced on the eleven o'clock news. What case you on?" he asks.

"Hit-and-run case involving Senator Brandon Caldwell's wife, Jacqueline," I reply.

Detective Fuller looks at me in astonishment. "You're not on that case, are you?"

"He came by my office today. He wants answers. What type of workup did you do for him with that murder?" I ask Fuller.

"Murder?"

"Yes, murder," I say.

Fuller snickers. "From what I know, it was an accidental hit-and-run. Just never caught the driver." He explains to me how the whole precinct was on the case for a month. The Virginia state troopers, the Virginia PD, and the FBI stopped every car resembling the description of the suspect vehicle from the borders of Washington, D.C., all the way to the Florida Keys. This was a high-profile case involving a senator's wife, so somebody had to pay. They scoured the whole South with forty-five officers from three districts and still came up empty. No partial plate ID. No surveillance footage from a bank camera or gas station. I mean, it was like a ghost hit this woman.

I open Fuller's draw and grab his ticket. "I'll bring it back if you hit, I promise," I tell him.

CHAPTER 4

I stroll up to the coroner's office to take a look at the photos of the victim. Mrs. Caldwell was a mess. The car literally ran her over. An eye had popped out of its socket from the back wheel rolling over her head. Her left foot got mangled in the muffler, and her arm was caught in the chassis. The accident twisted her ankle completely out of its joint. Scrapes and bruises from an eighteen-foot slide grated her skin to the bone before the car completely rolled over her. It was horrific.

A childhood friend of mine named Jimmy died from getting hit by a car. An '81 Trans Am speeding down 113th Avenue in Hollis, Queens, hit Jimmy and flipped him over the hood. He landed on his head. All the kids ran over to the scene while Jimmy just lay there with blood oozing out the back of his head. It had been an awful sight for an eleven-year-old to see. But Jimmy's body had still been intact. His eyes, his teeth, and his head were still whole. He even wore a slight smirk across his face like he'd died peacefully.

This hit-and-run on Jacqueline, though, this is something out of a horror movie. And what's more frightening, it wasn't an accident; it was done intentionally. I ask myself why I even need to see these pictures. But I have to. I want to feel the pain that Jacqueline's husband, Brandon Caldwell, is feeling. I want a reason to catch this killer. The squeamish feeling in the pit of my stomach from seeing the photos has turned my compassion for Jacqueline into anger at the perpetrator. Looking at the pics, I find myself taking this case personally, and I'm determined that someone is going to be brought to justice. The senator's wife dying is a very big deal.

Towards the end of the investigation, the Tenth Precinct came to the conclusion that it was a hit-and-run accident and the driver was long gone. Not me. That's not my conclusion. I turn and walk away, shifting my focus to the now rejuvenated Caldwell case.

CHAPTER 5

I take a long drive without Sandy in the passenger seat. When I got downstairs after viewing the photos, she was long gone. I wonder if she is suicidal and even think about going by her house to check up on her. But I can't; I have to get to Senator Caldwell's home. I can't get this case out of my mind.

I roll up to a circular driveway and am very anxious to see how a wealthy Senator lives. Soon as I enter this French Chateau Classical Renaissance-style brick castle, the first thing I notice is the huge picture hanging in the living room depicting Senator Caldwell and the current president, Barak Hussein Obama, posing with a congressional party behind them. On the far left wall there's a life-sized picture displayed of the senator in the White House Oval Office. More pictures of the senator at amusement parks with his wife and relatives. The senator's first catholic communion, his high school prom photo, a picture from his high school graduation, his Harvard Business School diploma, and a family tree. This wall depicts the senator's life from childhood to the present.

The senator walks in with a container of Tropicana orange juice in one hand and a DVD in the other. He wastes no time as he walks over to the DVD player and puts in the DVD. He picks up a remote and presses play. I anxiously wait to see what's going to pop up. Suddenly, it's street-view surveillance footage of an accident. Not just an accident, but *the* accident of Jacqueline Caldwell getting run over by a car. And as was stated in the written report, she has the walk signal. Mrs. Jacqueline Caldwell steps into the street and makes it past the first lane when suddenly a burgundy four-door sedan comes speeding at least seventy miles per hour and mows her down. My heart drops. Mr. Caldwell just stares at the screen, motionless, like he's seen this DVD a thousand times. It takes a lot for a man to become immune to seeing the murder of his wife. I feel kinda sorry for him but I can't help asking, "How did you attain a copy of this?"

He takes a sip of his juice. "You believe in God, Mr. Henderson?"

This is not the answer I was looking for, but I answer anyway. "Yes."

"You ever lose something or someone so close to your heart that it tests your faith?"

"Yes," I slowly answer again. "My German shepherd got hit by a car right in front of me when I was a seventeen. I prayed over him for forty-five minutes, asking God to please let him live. Then suddenly he just stopped breathing. Does that count?"

"What did that make you think of?" he asks.

I tell him, "Life and death belong in the hands of God. No matter what I wanted, God wanted something else. And who am I to question that."

He hits the play button again on the DVD player. We both sit silently watching the murder go down. Mr. Caldwell lets out a low grunt as the car hits his wife. By now the senator is in tears. He wipes his face and loosens his tie and takes a couple of big breaths. To tell the truth, I was sort of happy to see some kind of emotion come from him. It showed me that he still cared.

CHAPTER 6

It's late into the wee hours of the morning, and I decide to come home, leaving the senator drunk and sleeping on his butter-soft leather sectional. Coming through my wooden doors, I'm greeted by my dog, a male Rottweiler named Maxy. He's big and can eat a ton but still just a puppy, only in his second year. I rub his face with both hands and give him a hug around his neck. I do a jump shot with my keys into a toy basketball rim. Then I immediately go to my kitchen table, where the files on the senator's wife are resting.

I have a modern-style home that resembles my New York apartment. My interior is painted light green, and I have dark green wall-to-wall carpet. I put wooden tables at each end of a green leather sofa bed. Got my fireplace that hardly works in the living room. Deer Park watercooler in the kitchen. I wanted it to feel like I'd never left home. Not sure if that's a good thing, though.

I go to my refrigerator and grab a fresh bottle of Chardonnay and pour it into a four-ounce glass. I take a long sip. It's three thirty a.m., and my mind races with thoughts of how Sandy Lauson is doing. Though it's late, I decide I need to call to see if she ever made it home. Just a half-sleeping voice saying hello would be fine for me. I pick up my phone and dial. *Please pick up*, I think as the phone rings. I listen. No answer, just voice mail. I dial again but to no avail.

Finally, I just grab the files and open them. The word "DECEASED" sprawled right across the picture of Jacqueline Caldwell's face seems disrespectful to me. But she is dead. Monday, July 12, 2007, the deceased suffered a broken neck and severe hemorrhaging due to head trauma received on impact. At approximately Twelve-thirty-four p.m., the deceased was walking in the intersection of Main Street and Broadway and Lafayette in Fredericksburg, Virginia, when a four-door sedan blew through a red light and hit her.

As I flip through the pages, I see grainy surveillance photos from a couple of storefront cameras: Joe's Deli, Starbucks. Then there's one clean shot from the Union Bank and Trust Caroline County branch where Mrs. Caldwell was headed to meet an accountant to deposit her first lottery check. The shot shows an airborne Mrs. Caldwell. It sends chills down my spine. Then a further, clearer shot from a Chase Manhattan Bank branch about a quarter of a block away. This one shows the vehicle in traffic. Tinted windows. It even shows the vehicle getting in the far left lane. The sedan had no plates.

The report goes on to read that the husband was brought in for questioning. Not a suspect…yada, yada, yada. I take a long stretch, working out the tension of the day. Close the files and pull out my King James Version Bible and start reading. I've been reading the book of First Samuel, the story of how King David became a leader of the nation of Israel. What a journey it took for him to become king. Before I know it I am slow-blinking and falling asleep.

Suddenly, I enter into a dream state in which a bright light is coming from my kitchen and fully illuminating my house. As I watch, I see that the light is surrounding a human-like figure from head to toe. *It's an angel,* I think. Flashes of the movie *ET* also go through my mind. And just like clouds moving in the sky, this illuminated figure starts to glide across the floor. I am too afraid to even move. I'm not sure if I should bow down to this image or run. I struggle to get out a word, but I can't. Then, just like that, the image fades along with the light.

I wake up in a hot sweat and utter the word *"Dominic"* for some strange reason. My couch is drenched in sweat. I mean, I've had dreams and nightmares before, but this thing here moved my spirit. My heart is racing because it felt so real.

I look in the kitchen, and Maxy is just staring at me, panting heavily. "You saw it too, huh, boy?" I say to him. He runs over and jumps on my lap. Then I look at my clock. It reads 10:58 p.m. I can't believe I slept a whole day. I haven't done that since my college days. Then I realize it's lottery time. I quickly grab my remote and turn on my fifty-five-inch flat-screen TV to see exactly how this Powerball game is played. I just make it. A beautiful Indian woman comes on the screen and says, "Welcome to Wednesday's Powerball lottery drawing. Today's numbers are..." Then, one by one, white balls with black numbers on them come shooting out of an air-powered conveyor system. Twelve, twenty-four, thirty-four, fifty-five, thirty-three. Then a red ball with a single-digit number on it: eight. And that's it. For somebody, somewhere, life has possibly changed forever from that fifteen-second clip. *Wow*, I think. What a country we live in. With all the homelessness and poverty and starvation we have in this world, something as simple as plastic balls and a paper ticket can get you upwards of $200 million in any given week.

I grab my wine out the refrigerator. I'm still a little shaken from the dream I had. After one sip of my Chardonnay, it finally hits me, the word I said right after I woke up: Dominic. Sandy's son. I immediately grab my car keys and run out the house.

28

CHAPTER 7

I jump in my car and floor it, driving as fast as I can to Sandy's house. Suppose she killed her son and then killed herself. I mean, the stress in her face was enough to penetrate a steel mask. Then her seeing her husband in the precinct, lying through his yellow teeth, not giving a damn. Why wouldn't she want to off herself? Murder-suicides were becoming common as of late, and if I figure if I can do something to prevent one, I am going to damn sure try. She was about a half hour from my house, and I got there in eighteen minutes. Occasionally I use my police siren just to get a few open lanes when I need to.

I jump out my car and pound on Sandy Lauson's apartment door a few times, but I get no answer. I bang on it again. I can hear the steel screen door chipping at the termite-eaten wood frame. This time I call her name. "Sandy! Sandy, it's me, Garth, open up!" Still nothing. I go around to the back window and take a look inside. To see into the living room I have to look past the kitchen. But there is no light in the kitchen. Just an overhead in the upstairs staircase that's illuminating the living room. Then I look closer and I see Sandy lying on a couch with a pill bottle in her hand and a fifth of rum on the coffee table. *Oh my God*, I think.

Fearing the worst, I run back to the front door and kick it open. Almost brings me back to my robbery-homicide days in New York City when we used to kick open the doors of the dealers in Washington Heights. I hurry inside and immediately check her pulse. Then I shake her a few times. Saliva comes out her mouth. But it's not foamy and there's no vomit in it. Just saliva. "Sandy, come on. Wake up, baby. Snap out of it!" I desperately say. "Wake up!" I even give her a few hard slaps to the face, trying to shock her back to life.

Suddenly her eyes start to dilate and come into focus. She looks at me. I immediately ask her, "Where's Dominic, where's your son?" A tear rolls down her cheek. "What did you do to him?" I yell.

She wipes the slobber off her mouth. She looks at the medicine bottle on the floor. Speaking with the faltering cadence of an intoxicated person, she says, "I didn't take them. I thought about it, but I couldn't. He's not worth it."

"You didn't take these?" I ask, holding up the bottle of pills.

"No," she replies.

"Then what's wrong with you?" I ask, concern tinting my words.

"It's called drunk, Garth. Never seen a woman fall out drunk before, cop? Huh?"

"Where's Dominic?" I ask again.

"Sleeping, why? You think I would hurt him?"

I don't answer. I get up from the floor and go upstairs to Dominic's bedroom and stand over him. There he is, sound asleep, hugging a Cookie Monster pillow. I hear footsteps behind me, so I turn to see Sandy standing there, swaying.

"You think I would hurt my own son?" she angrily says, pressing her fist against her chest in defiance.

"Sandy, I'm not sure what you are capable of right now. You seemed distraught at the precinct. I just thought—"

"Thought what?" she quickly cuts in.

"You know, just thought you were ten-fifty-six. A lot has happened in the last two days, Sandy. I just couldn't risk it," I say.

Still fuming, Sandy stumbles over and gets right up in my face. "Risk what?"

I back up a little. Partly because of the flaming Bacardi breath and partly because I am standing over her son's bed and don't want to wake him, but mainly because she is a stunningly beautiful woman. Even in a sad, vulnerable state of inebriation, Sandy is a knockout. Her T-shirt and pajama bottoms do nothing to hide her curves. So I take a few more steps back, trying to be inconspicuous in my attraction to her.

"Look," I say, "I had a weird dream tonight. It kinda spooked me. I called your phone, you didn't answer. I banged on the door and didn't get no answer. I mean, I just thought something happened, that's all."

Sandy loosens up a little and follows me out the room. "You ever wish you could just start over?" she says.

"Maybe take back a bad day or two, but I've accepted the hand I was dealt, Sandy," I utter back. "You wanna start over, here's your chance. Your husband is gone, so here's your opportunity right now," I advise her.

She walks back downstairs to the kitchen. Fills up a glass with water from the faucet and gulps it down in one shot. "I envisioned a Cinderella lifestyle when I got married to Richard. Family trips, the latest model car every two years, summer beach house...now look at me. What a loser I've become," she somberly says.

This ordeal, her husband's wanting her murdered, is just too hard for her to bear. I have to think of a way to get this woman's thoughts back on track. If she wasn't suicidal before, she's sure starting to sound like it now.

"What about your son, your health? You're being selfish," I say.

"So?" she says.

"Look, you want some sort of counseling, I can get you some help. This ordeal has been way too much for you," I tell her.

"Ordeal? This is just a minor setback. My husband of eleven years hired you to kill me, that's all. I'm fine. I'm okay." She flops on the sofa. Starts to cry.

I sit down next to her and softly put my arm around her. She lowers her head into my chest. "Suppose I didn't get here in time? Suppose I was thirty minutes later? Would you have taken the pills?" I ask.

She shakes her head no in my chest. Her cries become even louder, almost sounding like high-pitched howls from a wolf. I offer her some more water. When I return with it and sit back down, she calmly takes a sip and wipes one of her tears.

"How did your wife die?" she asks.

"Giving birth. My son lasted two hours after her, then he died as well," I tell her. Tsst, well that explains it.

"How come you never remarried?" she continues.

I tell her she's not in the right state of mind to be having this conversation. I start talking to her about her son. Asking her questions about his upbringing. Did she ever take him to church? Is he circumcised? Does he read the Bible and know the Lord's Prayer? I can't help going back to the dream I had and wondering why I uttered Dominic's name when I came out of it. Maybe it was a sign of some sort. But all the answers she gives me don't make sense.

See, Sandy isn't a spiritual person at all. She was one of the fortunate beauties in her hometown of Fredericksburg, Virginia. Prom queen in high school. Cheerleader. Even won a few youth beauty pageants. In college she was the homecoming queen. Over three hundred signed entries in her yearbook. Voted as "*Most likely to make it in Hollywood.*" Yet she hardly ever prayed, neither was she a daily or even weekly reader of the Bible. Just went about life knowing right from wrong and using God-given common sense to get by.

I knew girls like her growing up. All beauty and no spirit. Some of them couldn't help it. It worked for them for so long, they didn't know any other way. From the time they were able to walk outside their mama's house on their own, men were offering them the world. Food, clothing, jewelry, shelter, transportation...you name it. When a person is in a position like that, she almost feels like she doesn't need God because she's given everything anyway. She starts to believe in that theory that says, "What is the sense of having God in my life? I'm quite okay on my own." It's only when ordeals, ordeals like Sandy's, come around that the girl starts to think, *Why me? Maybe I do need God.* But by then, most times it's just too late.

During a stretch in New York in the late nineties, when I was working the homicide division, I was on the Joel Rifkin serial killer case. Here's a guy who killed over seventeen women in New York City, dismembering their bodies and tossing them in the East River. He would do it right in his own sister's home. Most of them were prostitutes and drug addicts, of course. And I used to always wonder what would be going through a victim's mind as her neck was being crushed, while she stared at this murderer on top of her, breathing her last breath. In that moment, would she regret the choices she had made? Would she do it all over if she had another chance to live? When I looked at the photos of the women in their early years before they became prostitutes and drug addicts, they all seemed so young and pure, so beautiful and full of life with heads full of hair and pearly white teeth. What was it that made them choose their occupation, even when they knew the risks? I just couldn't figure it out.

It was no different when I thought about the adult entertainment industry. It really bothered me. Tons and tons of pretty young women becoming sexual deviants for a few hundred dollars a pop. I just couldn't figure out the *why* with women. So I started to just cast it off as them being part of the wicked cycle as well. And wicked people do wicked things, no matter how they look.

But Sandy is somebody the Lord put in my path for a reason. From the first time her husband, Richard, came to me in that bar, I said, "Thank you, Lord, for saving this one." If Richard had walked into any other bar, Sandy could've ended up just like one of Joel Rifkin's victims. *But why me and why now?* I think. It doesn't really matter; I have a case to close. A senator's wife has been murdered, and I need to get back to it.

CHAPTER 8

The next day I go to the Senate House of Commerce off of Main Street to see Senator Brandon Caldwell's day-to-day activities. Maybe he has enemies within his powerful circle of friends. I'm not leaving any stone unturned. As I look out into the main room, I see an auditorium filled with podiums and chairs. The room holds about 450 seats. They have bottled water and coffee and tea kettles sprawled about the place on the wooden tabletops. I spot Senator Caldwell sitting in a section that read "STATES LEGISLATIVE COMMITTEE of AMERICA."

After reading the sign on the door, I see that on today's agenda is an act banning partial birth abortions. It's been vetoed by the president, and the Senate is voting on an override. It's a typical day of the *Yea or Nay* vote, and each person has five or so minutes to get his point across and cast a ballot. The opposing parties include Planned Parenthood, a group that supports abortions and helps women have abortions if they feel they're not ready for children. Then you have other abortion activist groups like NARAL (National Abortion and Reproductive Rights Action League). This is a group of women that offers moral support, contraceptive information, and referrals to have safe abortions. In these organizations' views, it's up to the mother to decide.

The ban is being supported by the U.S. Bishops' committee for pro-life activities and Pro-Life America, groups that disapprove of birth control and contraceptives and abortion under any circumstances, including rape. They simply believe a woman has no right to kill what God has brought into this world. So needless to say, the tension in the room is high.

There are at least fifteen armed security guards on each floor. There are two bomb-sniffing dogs and, at least from what I can see, four secret service men in black roaming about with the ubiquitous earpieces and wrist microphones.

As I make my way to the upper level, I hear a commotion going on in the top tier not too far in front of me. Protestors are clashing with each other. Some religious groups tee off with the pro-choice organizations. A few hold signs that read, "What if God aborted you?" and "This is what a dead fetus looks like," with graphic pictures depicting a dead fetus on a metal pan in a clinic. Bibles are waved around as the shouting continues. Someone even splashes bottled water on a few of the protestors. Finally, the armed guards make it up to the top level. A few people are detained and some even handcuffed with plastic zip ties. It takes about five minutes before order is restored.

I sit down in my seat and watch Senator Caldwell as he calmly chats on his phone and types on his iPad. He is a Democrat, and it seems he is in the pro-choice section of the room. He takes a sip of his water and wipes his forehead. He speaks into the microphone.

"Good morning, ahh, Mr....excuse me, Cardinal Maida of Argentina, you have the floor, sir. Five minutes," he says.

Cardinal Conrad Maida of Argentina is fully dressed in his Catholic purple with a Pope-like crown on his head. He walks up to the microphone and taps it. "*Good morning, Mr. President. It is with great sadness that I note to you that the U.S. Senate, by a vote of fifty-seven to forty-one, has fallen short of overriding your veto of the Partial Birth Abortion Ban Act. Mr. President, I have received calls, joined in endless prayer vigils, and received millions of postcards from the American and Argentinean people, who have attempted to make themselves heard on this issue. The U.S. House voted to override your veto, but the Senate did not. We find this act ludicrous. Partial birth abortion is a particularly heinous and inhumane practice, which serves no medical or social purpose. To kill an infant who is just days, maybe even hours or minutes away from taking his or her first breath, is an unholy evil. Also, Mr. President, I, as a member of the U.S. Bishops' committee for pro-life activities, will travel to Washington, D.C. for another prayer vigil along with my brother cardinals, and we will persuade the members of the Senate to override your veto. For we are deeply disturbed at your latest juncture, and we will not stop until your veto is overridden. Thank you,"* the cardinal ends.

An applause rises up from the audience, completely drowning out the boos from the other side. The supporters of the cardinal's speech start stomping their feet on the floor in one accord. Senator Caldwell bangs on the microphone with two of his fingers, trying to quiet everyone. It causes a backlash of feedback, and a high-pitched screech whistles through the speaker system, causing the unruly audience to settle down.

Senator Caldwell grabs the microphone off the table and stands up. "Ladies and gentlemen, this is not a street demonstration. Please maintain order." He grabs a few papers out of his folder and takes a look at them. He looks around the room to the guest speaker section. "Now, the next speaker up is, ah, Cardinal Bevilacqua Decries of Mexico City, if I'm saying it correctly, sir."

The cardinal walks to the podium from his seat. Fully clothed in Catholic attire. Elderly man. Another Pope-like figure.

An altar boy in a black-and-white robe hustles up to the podium with a glass of fresh water. I can't help but to wonder whether this boy has been spoiled. And by spoiled I mean, you know, tampered with. It comes from my years in vice in NYC dealing with cases of molested kids from the Catholic church in the Lower East Side. I take a long look at the boy as he gives Cardinal Bevilacqua Decries his water. A tap on the top of his head says thank you. Cardinal Decries takes a sip and clears his throat.

As he leans into the microphone he looks around and waves to a nun in the front row. "*Mr. President, I am profoundly appalled over your veto of the Partial Birth Abortion Ban Act. I find it very sad when the president of this fine country endorses the killing of children that are in the process of being born. What does it mean in this country when they say, 'In God we trust'? When our unborn children can't be trusted in the hands of those who are supposed to deliver life? The culture of death is certainly upon us, Mr. President. In a world so filled with violence against children, it is incomprehensible that anyone could knowingly support such violence, particularly a president who has so often expressed concern for the welfare of this nation's young. I urge the U.S. Senate to please vote to override the president's latest veto and rid the earth of this extreme wickedness. Thank you.*" And just as with the last cardinal's speech, applause roars through the audience.

41

I notice Senator Caldwell slide his chair up to his microphone and loosen his tie as if he is preparing for battle. He's defiant in his speech. *"In the last two weeks we have been hearing and dealing with the battle of pro-life versus pro-choice. Pro-life forces have been promoting and printing misinformation, if not just flat out lying to you. The procedure we've all come to know as partial birth abortion is extremely rare in this country. They make up less than half of one percent of all abortions performed. Half of one percent. This subject only became an issue to the American people when a Mr. Ron Fitzsimmons, who was the director of the National Coalition of Abortion Providers, claimed there may be, and I emphasize the word 'may,' may be five thousand such abortions performed in the United States each year, if that."*

This goes on for about two hours, the powers that be fighting back and forth, and by this time, I've had enough. To me it is simple: as soon as a woman gets pregnant all bets are off. You lie down with a man and this is the result. But who am I, just a private eye looking for the killer of a senator's wife. However, the senator's being a pro-choice advocate kind of rubs me the wrong way. He is all for a fetus being aborted even up to the fifth month of growth in a woman's stomach. That's hard to me, somewhat barbaric. It takes a lot to digest an act like that. I often wonder how the doctors performing such a procedure can live with themselves. But there was the senator, arguing his cause with pride.

CHAPTER 9

I drive home *and happen to catch the rest* of the votes on C-SPAN. I lie back in my favorite lounge chair and hit my remote. Maxy must've been hungry while I was out because I see my garbage can on the floor, its contents forming a perimeter around it. When Maxy's been bad he doesn't come anywhere near me for a few hours. I have to lure him with some baked chicken just to get him to come out from under the dining room table.

As I turn up the volume on the TV, I hear Mr. Caldwell still at it, defending the laws of the land and his president's veto of the Partial Birth Abortion Ban Act. Tirelessly he continues his debate: *"And yes, I stand by my president's decision to veto the ban, not because I glamorize the issue, but because it is morally right. I'm a true believer in what the late Harry Blackmun said. A woman should have her God-given right to an abortion whenever she chooses, whether before three months or after five months. Women of this country should have this choice. That's what makes this country what it is—the freedom to practice your rights without worrying about politicians, religious leaders, or right-wing groups who want to bring harm to you for that practice. I mean, what is really at stake here? The fetus in a woman's womb is not yet human if it has not yet been born. This is not a murder being committed, people. This procedure saves more women's lives than—"*

Suddenly his speech is interrupted by another disturbance on the top level. I'm assuming the same unruly protestors from earlier in the day. A few cameras cut to the banners hanging from the top level. One reads: IF YOU BAN IT, WE WILL FIND A WAY. Another reads: 60,000 WOMEN DIE EVERY YEAR FROM SELF-MUTILATION ABORTIONS. Then footage of a tug-of-war between the banners. Things seem to be out of control in the auditorium. The TV cuts outside to a STOP THE MURDERS banner being set on fire. I turn my TV off. I have to think. Is there a connection between this abortion issue and the murder of the senator's wife? Or are the two things totally unrelated? If the senator is pro-choice, it doesn't mean his wife was. Or was she? I decide to look at the case from another angle.

CHAPTER 10

I decide I need to learn this whole lottery thing inside and out, so I pack a bag and take a road trip to West Des Moines, Iowa, to visit the Multi-State Lottery Association (MUSL). Maybe I can get answers from the people running Powerball.

When I arrive, I walk through a set of glass doors and find myself in the center of a beautiful marble and glass lobby. There is a beautiful sculpture of a round red Powerball with the number seven in the middle. They have a few Plexiglas photos of the Mega Millions announcer, Ralph Buckley, on the wall as well.

For a place that deals with handing out billions of dollars, I am pretty surprised at the lackluster security they have. Two guards at the front desk and one armed guard pacing the floor between the two sets of elevators. Maybe security is light because this place isn't a bank, though they do have checks. Big ones.

I walk to the directory and scroll down to the MUSL floor. There it is, fifteenth floor. I get on the elevator and am immediately joined by a beautiful blonde with a Starbucks coffee in her hand. Then an elderly couple, probably here to collect, steps on as well. I never could

46

figure out why these older people always seem to be the ones to win these big jackpots. I guess time and chance happen to us all.

I look at the blonde, wondering if she might have won the big game. "You win?" I say with a smile.

"Win what?" she fires back in a not-so-friendly voice.

"You know, the big one?" I say, trying not to be intimidated by her unfriendly response.

Finally, she smiles back. "No, I work here." She giggles. The elevator opens, and she steps off on the tenth floor. How stupid do I feel? I get to the fifteenth floor, step off, and take a look around the floor. There are about fifty cubicles and a drop ceiling with overhead fluorescents. The theme is an off-white and beige color scheme throughout the place. No real demographic in age of the workers I see. Young, old, black, white, short, tall, fat, and skinny.

I stroll over to the front desk. "Excuse me?" I say to the gentleman texting on his iPhone.

He pops his head up. "Yes, can I help you?" he asks.

I pull out my badge and push it just close enough for him to see it's a legit badge but not so close for him to read it's private sector.

"Garth Henderson. I'm looking for a Mrs. Terry Odgen. Where can I find her?" I say.

"Securities and integrity department down the hall. Five cubicles straight then make a left, go four cubicles, make a right, then three more down. She might be playing music," he answers.

"Thank you," I reply. I follow the yellow brick road he sends me on. Lefts and rights past cubicles filled with photos of family, dream vacations, boats, and cars tacked to everyone's walls. I approach Mrs. Terry Ogden's cubicle, and just like the receptionist said, she is playing music. Prince's "Purple Rain." Nice choice.

As I enter the cubicle, she turns in her chair. "Oooohh, you startled me," she says.

"Mrs. Terry Ogden?" I ask.

"Call me Terry. And you are?" she asks after scanning me up and down from head to toe, sizing me up.

"I didn't mean to startle you. Private Detective Garth Henderson. We spoke on the phone earlier this week. Can we talk?" I ask.

"Sure, let me find a room not so in the open." Terry leads me past a few more cubicle sections, then to a back conference room. She lowers the shades and turns up the lights on the dimmer.

She starts to explain to me the popularity of the lottery. "There are over one hundred and seventy-five million Americans playing this game. Fifty thousand venues to purchase tickets from. I'm surprised you never played Powerball," she jokes.

"I never said I didn't play, I'm just not a huge fan of the lottery. I'm from New York, and we didn't have the game until, I don't know, maybe a year or two ago. I'm a more of a quick-number-hit-type person. Win-4, the three numbers, and a few scratch-off win-for-life tickets. Buy for two and get four dollars back, you know, stuff like that," I answer back.

"We have twenty-one states involved in the Powerball lottery, and New York was the last state to finally get on board, in 2009, I believe. Started with eleven, then four more, then four more, you know," she says.

"Where does all the money go?" I ask.

"We divide it evenly between the twenty-one states. Every month all twenty-one board members get together and distribute a check between the winners and the states the game is played in," she answers.

"Is it profitable?" I reply.

"Almost twenty billion dollars to date, three billion to the winners…you tell me," she proudly says.

I start to think how much of a racket this country has going on with this lottery thing. Billions. I mean, there has to be some stealing going on in this business.

"I'm surprised New York took so long to get in on this. Wall Street. Financial capital of the world," I sarcastically say.

"Oh, New York has quite enough money, I'm sure," she says back.

I nod my head as if in agreement. Time to get down to why I came here in the first place now that I got her in a talkative mood. "So, you're the head of the securities and integrity department, right? You protect the winners?" I ask.

"Yes," she replies. Damn, suddenly the talkative Mrs. Terry Ogden has resorted to giving one-word answers.

"Were you shocked at Mrs. Caldwell's sudden death?" I ask.

"Certainly. Scared more like it."

"Scared?" I ask.

She gives me a look, like I shouldn't be surprised that she was scared. A few coughs and a finger slide through her hair later, she clarifies the statement. "We don't want our winners getting murdered, Mr. Henderson. And the fact that she had chosen to remain anonymous was even more troubling. But when we heard it was a hit-and-run, it eased us a little. As opposed to being shot or stabbed, you know, something more intentional."

I investigate even further. "So you weren't sure how she was killed at the time?" I ask. My line of sincere questioning seems to have eased Terry back into a talkative mood.

"Well, an officer contacted us from the Virginia PD and explained to us that, ah, Jacqueline Caldwell had been killed."

I ask her what officer, but she can't remember. I stay in the room with Terry for over an hour as she explains to me how a detective from Virginia had contacted her since and told her that it was a hit-and-run accident. He didn't know the make and model of the car. He hadn't even told Terry if Jacqueline was walking, riding a bike, or in a car herself. He just initially told her she was killed by an automobile accident. I ask whether she had met Mrs. Caldwell. She says yes and compliments her on how nice of a woman she was. I write down everything on a yellow pad.

"So," Terry goes on to say, "Jacqueline came up here to receive her winnings on a Monday and went back to Virginia to meet with an accountant at Union Bank and Trust to deposit the check when she was unfortunately killed. She took the long-term plan. I believe it was a little over five million dollars a year for twenty years, excluding taxes."

"So what bothered you about the way she was killed or the case?" I ask.

"Well, it's really not my place to say, but I understand her husband is into politics, a senator or something," she whispers.

"And that bothers you?"

Terry slightly nods her head. At this point she's squirming around in her chair in an uncomfortable fashion. I personally can't understand how Jacqueline's husband's being a senator would bother a lottery commission employee, but I just figure she doesn't trust politicians. However, what bothers me is that the lottery commission has held back the money from going to next of kin. Which in this case is the husband.

Senator Caldwell hasn't received a dime of the winnings. I have to find out why.

"So I'm guessing you guys up here in Iowa don't trust politicians?" I ask.

"Of course we do, Mr. Henderson," she smirks.

"Yeah, because every time I watch the presidential race, this is one of the states that every candidate must win, right? Iowa, caucus state or something, yeah? So I know you guys are into politicians. So what was the problem with Senator Caldwell? Why did you dispute Jacqueline's last will and testament and pass her case to a probate judge? You prompted an investigation?" I say, intent on getting answers.

Terry goes defensive. I can almost see the hairs on the back of her neck rise, like a cornered feline's.

"Well, it wasn't just me," she says. "The whole securities and integrities committee agreed on this. The police were calling every day. I just personally don't trust politicians, Mr. Henderson. Never have." She starts fixing her hair after losing her cool for a moment. "I mean, it shouldn't be so easy for the next of kin or the beneficiary to receive that much money without some kind of investigation. Especially after a mysterious death," she says.

"And why were you contacted, or how, I should say more like it?" I ask her.

"By phone. My guess is the MUSL lottery check was in her possession at the time of death."

This bothers me. Thinking of Jacqueline having a check for $5 million in her possession. The suspect list could jump to a thousand people just on that alone. This day and age, with this economy, who wouldn't kill for that type of money?

"That's your security for winners, to walk around with five-million-dollar checks in their pockets? Why not electronic money or wire transfer, something like that?" I ask Terry.

Her reply doesn't ease me at all. "To each their own, Mr. Henderson. She wanted a check, we gave her a check."

I ask Terry if I can see the will. She goes over to the next office and pulls the files from off of a table. She opens a manila folder and pulls out a copy of the will and shows it to me. "Here's a copy," she says.

"And the original?" I ask.

"In probate, with the New York Supreme Court," Terry replies.

I start to look over the will, reading the wording carefully. Notations. Signing. Everything must be examined with close attention with these things, including looking over the fine print. Mr. and Mrs. Caldwell had no children, and neither had living parents. Senator Caldwell is definitely the beneficiary. So I can't see him as a strong suspect in her murder anymore. He's the next of kin, and besides that, they both would have shared the winnings. They were married, for goodness sake. What's hers is his, vice versa. *Why kill her?* I think to myself. It just doesn't add up. I don't see enough of a motive for Senator Caldwell to have had his wife whacked before she even had a chance to deposit the check.

Terry stares at me the whole time I am reading the copy of the will, trying to read my demeanor. She sees with my constant head shakes of denial and deep sighs. "Maybe he was a greedy man that didn't want to share. Maybe politics played a part. You know how those heathens are in Washington," she utters.

I shoot back, "I met her husband, and prick that he is, he didn't seem money hungry, Mrs. Ogden. Senator Caldwell comes from money, did you know that? His family is kin to Charles Gulden. You know who that is?" I ask.

"I'm assuming the Gulden's mustard people," she replies.

"Yes," I say. "He never even asked about her winnings. He just wanted to find his wife's killers."

Terry takes a long breath. I can tell she's had enough of me. "You could never tell off of a first meeting, Mr. Henderson. The wickedness in the hearts of men goes way beyond first impressions, believe me."

I look Terry in the eyes after this statement. Maybe she's right. Maybe I am being played by the senator? She's made an interesting point. "You're right," I say. "It's hard to judge anyone these days."

Terry also tells me that Mrs. Caldwell wanted to open up a daycare center and children's hospital in Virginia for the Haitian refugees that were coming over from that devastating earthquake.

"So what happens now?" I ask.

"The Multi-State Lottery Association only takes orders from the courts on probate cases like this. We have nothing to do with the outcome. Once the word comes from the probate judge after the hearings, that the senator is clear, we will enact the will of Jacqueline Caldwell with no problem, along with sending an apology letter to the senator. He'll be one hundred and ten million dollars richer, so I don't think he'll be too put out." Terry gets up to leave, and I quickly open the door for her. I look at Terry to say something but hold my tongue.

I reach out my hand, and after a slight pause, she reaches hers out and we shake.

"Do you mind if I make a copy of this will?" I ask. She nods okay. "Thank you for your time, Mrs. Ogden," I say to her.

"Please, call me Terry. After all, we're friends now, right?" she fires back.

"Well, since we're friends, do you got a tip on the next set of numbers coming out?" I jokingly ask.

She laughs. "Luck of the balls, Mr. Henderson, just the luck of the balls." I walk out.

CHAPTER 11

I have a long drive home, but it's good because it gives me time to try to figure out this case and everything that Terry told me.

When I get home I have an e-mail alert on my computer. It seems there was a hit-and-run accident in New York City. It happened in the middle of the afternoon on a crowded downtown street called Chambers. Not too far from the Brooklyn Bridge. This is also the major courthouse district in the city as well. Two men were having lunch around noon. Nothing special. Just pizza and sodas. Suddenly, out of nowhere, a speeding car came flying down from Broadway and slammed into both of them at top speed. Witnesses say they never even heard a screech. No horns blowing, no screams to get out the way, just *boom*! Both men flipped over the hood and went airborne. An ambulance came and pronounced both men dead at the scene.

I read the e-mail again just to see if I missed anything. I'm thinking because I've been searching hit-and-run murders all this past week that this just happened to come in through my search engine updating service. I don't pay it much mind.

Later on, I go to pay Sandy Lauson and Dominic a visit at Saint Luke's Hospital in downtown Virginia. Sandy took my advice and got Dominic circumcised. I sit in Dominic's recovery room for hours watching a thirteen-inch color TV. *Mash* reruns and *Matlock* and a few cartoons. Dominic sleeps the whole time.

After a while, I walk around the hospital a few times looking for Sandy, but I can't find her. Flirt with a few cute nurses mulling around the children's hospital and even score a telephone number that I probably won't even use. Sometimes I just like to see if I still got it. I'm bored and just killing time.

I go back to Dominic's room and grab the Gideon Bible that they have in the bedside drawer of every hospital room. I myself am an avid King James Bible reader. These new versions change everything to fit the culture that we're living in, and I don't like that. I just can't seem to understand why you need a new translation from English to English. It doesn't make sense. Changing the words takes away the true meaning of the words. But the Gideon has to do for now.

After reading for a bit, I turn on the TV and flip to C-SPAN. Lo and behold, another political debate going on between pro-choice and pro-life. This is a hot topic this election year. I quickly turn the TV off in disgust.

Soon after, a doctor walks in. Tall, handsome fella with a slicked blond hairstyle. This guy looks like he could've been a ball player or an Olympic swimmer in his past. Six foot five at least. His nametag reads: *Doctor Pilsario, Pediatrics.* I stand up to greet him with a firm handshake just to let him know size doesn't matter. I even deepen my voice a tad bit.

"Good afternoon," he greets me. "And you are with the mother, Sandy Lauson?" he asks.

Quickly I reply, "Yes, how is Dominic?"

But instead of answering me, he pushes even further on my identification. "Are you the husband, boyfriend, relative?"

Now, I'm thinking he's fishing for one or two reasons. One, he's trying to protect the child, being that this has become a pedophile society and you just can't take any chances on strangers, or two, he's trying to lay with a beautiful single mom whose son just had surgery and he needs to find out if I'm in the way. Now that he's pushed, I figure I'll play around with him a little. "Husband, yeah, I like that title. I'm the husband," I sarcastically say with a smile. "So how is he?" I ask again.

"He's doing fine. He'll be asleep for another two hours or so." Dr. Pilsario takes a look at his Audemars Piguet wristwatch. Seems to me like he's just flashing his bank account. "But he'll be very drowsy from the anesthesia. Now it is very important that he drinks large quantities of water the first few hours after waking." Then the doctor hands me a list of things to look for and other stuff that Dominic has to do as he recovers.

My feelings are leaning toward just waiting for Sandy at this point. Technically, I am not the father. I take a look at the list. It explains the stinging sensation Dominic will have upon urinating for the first time. He has to drink lots of water, yada, yada, yada. So I cut to the chase. "How long for the kid to heal, Doc?" I ask.

"Two to three weeks before he'll have some sort of normalcy. Scabbing will go away then you bring him back here for the bandages to be removed. He'll be fine." The doctor hands me some pills and a prescription to fill.

"Thank you, Doctor Pilsario, right?" I say.

"Yes, Pilsario. I've been meaning to ask you, Mr., um…I'm so bad with names." Payback. Just like a child.

"Garth," I say.

"Garth, yes. I usually don't ask, but most parents bring their children in for circumcision at a very early age, maybe before their first birthday, or very late, like after their twelfth. I personally have never done a four-year-old. Two years old at most. What was it that drove you two to bring the little one in?"

"The kid is special, Doc. And he ain't gonna be shortchanged by this society," I quickly reply. Not that it is any on his business.

The doctor smirks at me. He still seems a little confused about me keeping the laws of Moses. I mean, it is a rare practice nowadays. But he takes my answer for face value. "Well, God bless you and the little one," he says.

"Same to you, sir."

The doctor leaves the room. I take a stroll over to Dominic, still thinking about that dream I had a week ago in my living room. Then suddenly I hear a voice. "How is he?" the woman's voice says. I turn and it's her, Sandy Lauson. *Wow,* what a change. Sandy looks reborn. Her hair is done up in a burgundy wash. Her lips are glossy with red lipstick. She's sporting a bright red dress, and if I can frankly say, she looks stunningly beautiful.

"He's fine," I say. Still staring at her lip gloss. I hand her the medication and the prescription receipt. "Just make sure he takes his medication."

Sandy shows me a bottle of her own pills in her hand. I take a look at them. Antidepressants. Zoloft and Paroxetine. If I remember correctly, these are suicide-prevention drugs. So that's where she went, to see a shrink. "Doctor said I just need to relax a little. Take these for a few weeks and I'll be fine," she says.

I quickly change the topic back to Dominic. "So the doctor gave me these, Sandy." I hand her an application to fill out and explain to her the dos and don'ts and what to look out for during her son's healing process. While I'm explaining the daily routine I catch a whiff of her perfume. Damn, this woman is going be my downfall. I slowly back off. It's hard to even look her in the eyes.

"Thank you, Garth. You've really been there for us," she says.

An uncomfortable silence descends on us as I look at her. Trying to keep myself under control. I've always been like this. Truth is, I have a lust demon inside of me that won't go away. It's been years since my vice squad days with my old partner in Hell's Kitchen. There were so many prostitutes and so many night crawlers. We racked up points with hookers, strippers, and runaways who owed us for their freedom.

I was young and reckless, fresh on the force with a team of wild cowboys that ran the Times Square area in the eighties. And though I buried that demon deep, deep down in the pits of my old selfish flesh, it still just hovers around in my mind, waiting for an opening. Sometimes fighting it off leads me to blurt out things at the wrong time, like a schizophrenic talking to himself on the subway. I quickly inhale.

"Sandy, let me be honest with you, I can't allow myself to get too close to a business-related acquaintance...or a married woman, especially one as beautiful as you, without having covetous feelings. I know what you've been through these last couple of weeks, and I know you don't consider yourself married anymore, but in the eyes of the Lord and the law, until you get that bill of divorce from Richard, you still are. So I'm gonna stay clear from you until that's taken care of."

After that long-winded outburst, I don't know what to expect from her. I just hold my breath. Sandy just stares at me. Seductively blinking her eyes as if what I said has turned her on even more. What did I just do? Then she inhales, causing her breasts to rise, pulling the red dress even tighter as she does so. She strokes her hair back from out of her face, but there's one strand that's become caught on her glossy lips. She pulls that strand as well. Licks her lips.

"I'm single, Garth," she says. "Been that way for a while. Me and the asshole haven't been intimate for years. I removed my emotion from the relationship just to get by. Occasionally I would give in to intimacy, thinking it would bring Richard and me closer together, but it didn't. And as much as he hated me for that he couldn't leave. My beauty has always done that for men. Now you, I see it in your eyes, Garth. You desire me but you're under some sort of religious restraint. I understand. I'm irresistible. There's no shame in that," she says while walking closer to me.

"I, on the other hand, am a woman. I work off emotion. I want to somehow repay you for saving my life. You could have taken the money Richard paid you to kill me and no one would have known. Did you ever think about it?" she asks.

"Never." Just the thought of someone's life being worth ten grand rubs me wrong. Even though you can take out a hit on a person for fifty bucks these days with these junkies, I just couldn't do it.

"You think ten thousand dollars is worth someone's life?" I ask.

"To some it is, even less. But you didn't. And for that, I'm willing to repay you in any way or any position possible," she says, almost in a whisper. "Any way you want, sir".

My jaw almost drops. She's gone and conjured up that demon I try so hard to suppress. I'm speechless. At least forty-five seconds must pass. Maybe my carnal side is actually weighing the pros and cons of this offer. Suddenly, I snap out of it.

"Sandy, I can't," I say. "That's you and your thyroid condition talking. I was just helping you get yourself together and get your son right. A thank you is sufficient enough," I tell her.

"You were a New York City cop, right?" she asks.

"Yes, twenty-six years," I tell her.

"How did you do it?"

"Do what?"

"Manage to stay uncorrupted after being around all that poison?" she says.

"At first I didn't. I was a venomous snake spewing out poison like the rest of the serpents, just trying to balance out the universe with the just and the unjust. Then, the Lord happened," I tell her.

"The Lord, huh! NYPD...you can't tell me you've never been tempted. Even Jesus was tempted by Satan. Why did you leave the force?" she tenaciously asks as if I'm under interrogation.

I quickly correct her. "Jesus wasn't tempted at all but Satan tried to tempt him and failed."

"Did you quit?" she says.

"I was fired if you must know." I tell her the story of the straw that broke the camel's back. That camel being me and my job at the NYPD's vice squad division. That's when I transferred to homicide.

CHAPTER 12

It was a warm night. Summer, I believe. Me and my old partner, Waxton Alverez, Wax for short, were making rounds. He was a twenty-five-year-old Puerto Rican playboy from the Lower East Side's Alphabet City. Had the ladies going crazy around the clock. This kid could score a lay no problem on any given day of the week.

Anyway, we got a 1034 (assault) call from a woman in distress screaming down in the LES (Lower East Side). Back then folks didn't have cell phones, Android devices, or cameras, none of that. You got a call on your radio, you had to investigate, see what was going on. Wax was all juiced up because this call came from his home turf. And one thing he hated were criminals roaming around where his mama, wife, and kids laid their heads. He was banging on the roof of the Cutlass Ciera with his fist. Rocking back and forth in his seat and shaking his knees like a madman. His method for dealing with perps in his neighborhood was simple. And by simple I mean he'd kick them off the planet. Kill 'em. He'd had already three good shoot-outs, two of which resulted in the perpetrators' dying.

So Wax was flying down First Avenue, taking red lights like he was on I-95. We arrived about seven minutes after getting the call. We entered this building right off of Second Street and Avenue A. Wax barged in with two guns out. That was his trademark. *"Always have a backup gun in your hand, Garth. Fuck is it gonna do buried on your ankle,"* he would always tell me.

So we crept in the doorway of a dimly lit hallway. You could smell the piss reeking from the elevator as soon as you stepped inside. Rat feces and stray dog stench everywhere. We climbed up one flight of stairs. An old woman, looked to be in her late seventies, cracked open her apartment door. She pointed down with her wrinkled shaking finger to apartment 5X. Then she quickly closed her door.

I pulled my weapon. Wax already had both of his up. A Glock 17 9mm and a silver .380 Magnum. We both book a breath. Adjusted our bulletproof vests. Wax put his ear to the door and listened. We could both hear a low moan coming from inside. Almost as if someone had a pillow over their mouth or duct tape wrapped around their lips. Something was smothering their cries for help. Then we both heard a strange noise followed by a smothered scream.

Wax wasted no time reacting. He took half a step back and, BOOM!, kicked the door open with the uttermost force, causing the overhead light fixture to shatter. We burst into the room, and to our shock, we saw a young girl, couldn't have been no older than sixteen, tied to a bed post. Bound and gagged with silk stockings from end to end. Her mouth had a stocking *in it. Her feet were being held down by a voluptuous woman dressed in only thong panties. Her face was buried in this young girl's vagina. The girl's face was red and she had welts all over her body. You could tell she was taking a beating.*

But what was more shocking was another woman lying under this girl with her arm wrapped around the girl's neck. She was kissing her in her ears. There were various sex toys laid out on the bed and a bottle of syrup or honey of some sort. A bottle of Hennessy Black was also on the table. I took a deep breath.

Wax had already broken off to secure the rest of the apartment. I heard him yelling "Clear!" every few seconds as he scanned each room. Finally he came out of the last room with a smirk on his face. I immediately went over to the bed and pulled the stocking out of the young girl's mouth. She immediately blurted out, "Help, I'm being raped. I was kidnapped!" I grabbed the woman that had her hands around the young girl's neck and pulled her out from under the girl and gave her a little toss to the floor.

The other one stood up. "She's lying. She's a whore and we paid for her," she said.

I finished untying the fragile girl. She ran over to her clothes and hid behind me and started crying as she was dressing. I took a look around the room, which resembled an S&M chamber, then into the eyes of the victim.

70

Young, slim, fragile. She was terrified, and I knew she was telling the truth. This was rape. Both suspects looked at Wax and me with distain, still possessed by whatever demons that had led them here in the first place. I couldn't hold it in any longer. I had raised a girl before and so did Wax. These girls were disgusting diseases.

"Where are you from?" I asked the young girl.

"Montana, here to see my aunt. This lady said she would give me a lift from the Port Authority. Then they brought me here," she cried back.

By now my hand was shaking. Wax was still indecisive on what to do. For a second I thought I saw one of the women wink at Wax, almost as if she was tempting him to join in. He gave me a side look for approval, but he knew there was no way out of this for these damn rapists.

That's at the top of my list of crimes I hate. Rape, male or female. Being on vice squad for so many years, I got to see it all. Most people think of rape as something that only happens to a woman by a man. But in my line of work, you learn that it damn near evens out between rapes of men, women, and children.

"On your knees, hands on top of your head!" I ordered the two women.

They slid off of the bed. One wiped her mouth, still shiny with saliva from her efforts with the girl. She looked at Wax and smiled. Then turned to me. "We're finished with the cunt anyway. You two perverts can have her now."

At that moment, something came over me. That judge, jury, and executioner feeling that I get from time to time had returned. It's an overwhelming state that I go into when I get angry, completely taking over all of my senses. Almost like the Incredible Hulk, except I don't turn green, my muscles don't grow, and I don't bulk up to 365 pounds of pure adrenaline. But something does happen. Maybe I have a split personality. Maybe I have blackouts. All I know is when it happened that night, I shot that woman point blank in the stomach. I had no feeling at all about it either.

***

I finish my story and look up at Sandy. By now she is staring at me like I need a Zoloft.

"Did you kill her? Sandy asks.

"No. But her days of raping children were over," I tell her. I get up off of Dominic's bed and grab my coat. "I just wanted this sodomizing woman to know what pain felt like for that moment," I nonchalantly say to Sandy.

Sandy doesn't say a word after that. She just stares at the floor, avoiding eye contact. I'm sure how she feels about me anymore. This story takes me back to the second meeting I had with Richard, Sandy's husband, at the same bar. Another cash deposit on the hit. This time we had a brief conversation. When I'd asked him, why did he want to have his wife killed, he told me he was tired of his sacrifice, of not being appreciated. He'd called Sandy selfish. He said he wanted her to feel the same pain he did. It takes a lot of effort to hate so bad that you want to see the person dead. But that is how he felt at that point in his life. This man was extremely angry and felt scorned more than any woman could ever be. He'd even asked to watch the murder go down from a parking lot across from the crime scene. I'd convinced him that seeing a loved one die and hearing the screams and the blood-curdling cries of his wife would haunt him forever. He'd taken a minute before he changed his mind.

As I leave the hospital room, I tell Sandy, "Matthew six and nine." She looks at me, not too sure about what I am talking about. "The Bible, teach Dominic the book of Matthew chapter six and verse nine. It's the Lord's Prayer. He'll love it," I say. She nods okay.

CHAPTER 13

I'm back home with my dog, Maxy, pouring out Science Diet dog food into a big blue bowl. These Rottweilers can eat. Maxy is so hungry, he can't even wait. He's chomping down and splashing food all over the place while I'm pouring. Has it been that long since I've been home? I walk into my bedroom, which has a color-coded organization to it. Green is one of my favorite colors. I have a green queen-sized quilt on my bed. My walls and carpet are green as well. Even my night tables are green. But they're all in different shades, of course. It puts me in an outdoors, forest-type mood.

So I jump in my bed, and right on cue Maxy jumps in with me. He has his own place right at the bottom of my feet. I have a nice little blanket set up for him. I reach in my drawer and grab a few pictures out from my hit-for-hire case of Sandy Lauson. Still haven't figured her out yet. I flip through a few pages and toss them on top of the night table. I have to get my head back in the game. I can't get too wrapped up in Sandy Lauson, her thyroid condition, or her son. But I have to look at her photos just one more time. Sometimes the devil lurks at the most vulnerable hour of the day. It is two a.m. You have to always be on guard when dealing with the devil because he doesn't get tired and he never quits. My carnal flesh is screaming to call Sandy as I take a glance at my phone, but my spiritual side brings me back to my senses: she's still a married woman and I'm not an adulterer. I must wait. Even though my testosterone level is peaking from our earlier meeting in the hospital, I feel the need to win this war between the flesh and the spirit. *Ah, hell with it, I'm gonna give her a call just to say goodnight,* I think, knowing I'm slowly losing the battle.

I reach for the phone, but it rings before I can pick it up. Wow, maybe it's her. Oh wait, that's not my phone. *Ring, ring again.* It's my doorbell. I get up and quickly fix myself. I grab a wooden brush from off my dresser and pull it through my hair. I must look presentable. Especially considering the way Sandy looked the last time I saw her with her son. The doorbell goes off again.

"Just a minute," I yell toward the door. I hustle over to the door but not before taking one last look in the mirror. I'm good. I finally open the door with half a smile, yearning to see Sandy's beautiful face. Then...

"Senator Caldwell, how did you find my home?" I say in disgust while I glance at my watch. The senator walks in right past me without uttering a word. Damn near pushes me against my door as he flies by. I'm fairly disappointed to the point of it being readable on my face, and I don't care. I want him to know he is *persona non grata* in my home. Judging by the senator demeanor and countenance, he wants me to know that he doesn't care.

"So how far are you?" he quickly asks.

"Senator, it's two in the morning, these are not my working hours."

"How far, Garth?"

"From what?" I ask.

"Solving my wife's murder."

I finally close my door. "You're a Democrat, a pro-choice Democrat at that. How could you be for partial birth abortion? Don't you know the baby is alive in the womb?" I say while glaring at him.

"I wasn't aware of your sudden interest in politics," he nonchalantly says with a slight head bobble.

"Not really an interest. I just happened to hear your speech on C-SPAN the other day and it made me sick to my stomach," I tell him.

"There are two sides to every story, Mr. Henderson. Half of the country loves me for what I'm doing—protecting their rights, free will, and liberty to buy assault weapons, chew tobacco, or legalize marijuana. The other half would rather see me dead, just like those unborn children you feel so sympathetic about. I'm just doing my job."

After a small chuckle, I shake my head in amazement. "Job! You're polluting the earth, Senator. You're no different from those bastards performing honor killings in Iran and Afghanistan on women that were victims of rape."

The senator gives no reaction to my last comment. I almost feel like a child when he asks his mother who she's on the phone with and she keeps on talking without even acknowledging the question. The senator quickly goes back to why he is paying me in the first place.

"Anyway, Garth, where are you with finding my wife's killers? Should I be getting another private investigator?"

I let the senator know that I took a trip to the Multi-State Lottery Association. I also tell him about his being the beneficiary to his wife's estate. And though he hasn't yet seen his wife's last will and testament, he doesn't seem surprised. I guess he figures he's the husband, so why not.

Just out of curiosity, I flat out ask him, "What were you two gonna do with all that money?"

Suddenly, the senator gets up and walks into my kitchen. He looks to the right and notices Maxy standing there, staring at him. Senator Caldwell opens the refrigerator and grabs a bottle of Chardonnay. "My kind of man," I hear him mumble under his breath.

I walk into the kitchen behind him and get a wine glass out of the cabinet. He pours us two glasses. Suddenly, I'm feeling like a guest in my own home. The senator walks back into the living room and takes a seat in my favorite reclining chair. *How much of this can a man take?* I think to myself. Then he drops a bombshell on me. "I was going to drop out of next year's Senate race and run for president. The money my wife received from the Powerball winnings was going to fund a strong two-year-long campaign that would have pretty much assured me a victory."

Straightaway I feel a tingling sensation going up my spine. This case has just taken a turn and suddenly I'm in the big leagues.

"Presidency!" I say. "You think your plan leaked and someone wanted to stop you?"

He takes a sip of wine. "Leaked how? I was still a year and a half away from my Senate term ending. Besides, Jacqueline and I both made a solemn promise to keep it a secret. That's why she remained anonymous about her winning lottery ticket. No one knew about it outside of the police at the Tenth Precinct," he tells me.

"And the Powerball committee," I quickly shoot back.

His countenance grows bitter. "Yeah, them," he vehemently says. "They couldn't seize the money fast enough. What were their views on the matter?" he asks.

I tell him that the case is out of their hands. The money is in probate court. I let him know that a probate judge has to rule on his innocence of the murder, and what they will do is contingent on the outcome of a hearing.

The senator isn't really interested in hearing any of it. As far as he is concerned, everyone thinks he is guilty of murdering his wife. I can only imagine how it feels to walk around with such a label tagged on you, especially if you're innocent. Then he drops another bombshell.

"You know by law they have three more days to make that decision, and then the Multi-State Lottery Association has to resume sending me the checks. One year after the investigation started."

To my surprise, I almost drop my wine glass. "I didn't know that," I reply, surprised.

"I also happen to know the probate judge in charge of my wife's case. Being a senator has it perks," he says.

"I bet you it does." The hairs on my neck start to rise. "Do you know the judge's verdict, too?" I candidly ask.

"Never bothered to call," he tells me. "I didn't want to complicate matters more. Just think of what they would say if they thought I coerced the judge's ruling."

I can't figure out if it was the money the Senator was after or if he wanted to clean up his image to get a clean run for the presidency. It's one thing if you run for president after being recently widowed, because you can gain a lot of support just on sympathy alone. But if you run for president and they think you killed your wife and, on top of that, used her Powerball winnings to fund your campaign, well, there's just so much American voters can take.

"What is it you want, Senator? Why did you come here at this late hour?" I ask.

"I feel somewhat guilty for my wife's murder, Garth, especially if politics played a part. She always stood by me. I can't sleep at night. I need to know why they did it. I need closure." The senator takes another sip of his wine followed by a full-on gulp, finishing it. He looks at me, knowing I have a few questions to ask him, but he beats me to the punch. "I know what you're thinking, why they, plural, right?" he asks.

I slowly nod a yes.

He gets up. "I want you to come by my house this weekend. I have something I want you to see," the senator tells me.

I am hesitant at first because I don't want to walk into any political snafus. Coming from New York, I know you have to stay five steps ahead of your enemy, and politicians are people I consider enemies. Besides, this case is starting to intimidate me in the worst way. I am scared. It is big now. It doesn't take a genius to figure out I am way out of my league and getting deep into an area of investigation that I'm not familiar with nor do I want to be. With political scandals you have agencies like the Secret Service, FBI, and CIA dealing with things, which for the most part are all government-controlled police organizations. They are threatening to an extent but they still have a boss that they have to answer to.

It's those ubiquitous black tie and suit-wearing characters you see in movies that you have to worry about. Those spooks, spies, and men in black are the ones that really terrify me. If a senator's wife was murdered and it was politically motivated, I really don't want to be part of it. These off-the-book, black op groups fight extremely dirty. They're known to spray a drop whatever solution in your drink while you're not looking in a bar or plop a drop of cyanide in your hair and three days later you're in a coma or cardiac arrest. I saw the picture of the former KGB agent, Alexander Litvinenko, in *Time*. They labeled him a Russian spy. He was sprawled all over the BBC and the UK newspapers with sunken, dark eyes, a premature balding head, and yellow skin. It was a very stark image that showed what it's like to be poisoned and clinging to life in a British hospital. When you looked up this man's life, just three weeks before, he was a happy, healthy man with a full head of hair, jogging five miles a day. Then, boom, a week later he was deteriorating in some quarantined section of a hospital with plastic drapes surrounding his bed and doctors fixing him with blank stares.

I do not want to end up like Alexander, but here I am, small-time private investigator, Garth Henderson, getting in too deep where I don't belong. I agree to go by the senator's house this weekend anyway, though I know this case could possibly kill me. I just have to see what he has in hopes of closing this murder mystery. Truthfully speaking, I was already too far spent when the senator walked through my doors with that manila envelope. There's no turning back now. Maybe I should write a will as well.

The senator has the decency to take his glass and put it in the kitchen sink. I look at Maxy, who is still sitting there not making a sound.

"Never have I seen a dog so disciplined," the senator says.

"He doesn't get too friendly with people he doesn't trust," I tell him.

The senator quickly laughs off my comment. "Can I ask you a personal question?" I prepare for anything as I nod with a slow blink. "I hear you were at vice in New York for six years, then went to homicide for seven."

"Eight," I quickly reply.

"Sleazy sex crimes to murder…why? Did you expect a change for the better?" he asks.

"See you been checking up on me," I say.

The senator smiles then shrugs. "Just curious about a man that makes a move like that. Usually it's from vice squad to a new job, not homicide."

I stare at the senator and don't offer a word, but he's not budging. The man wants answers. I tell the senator a story about my last year at vice and what went down to make me switch from vice to homicide.

"It was spring '92 and I was doing surveillance on a tenement building in Harlem. A rapist was preying on dancers of the night coming from two adjoining strip clubs off of the West Side Highway. The Golden Circle and Naughty Boy were the names. He would snatch his victims coming off the late shift and then hit the highway. Not really sure how he would get them in the car, but I'm thinking stun gun. Most of them would be found under the George Washington Bridge the following day with marks all over their bodies.

"So I was casing both joints for six hours and it was starting to turn daylight. I was dead tired and in between dozing off when I decided to call it a night. Suddenly I see a man come running by my car, profusely sweating with a petrified look on his face. He was sporting a T-shirt and boxers that were also fully drenched. Then about fifteen yards behind him was another man toting a double-barrel Remington shotgun. It was a long sucker, too. He was chasing this guy down Twelfth Avenue from out of the Taft housing projects.

My natural instinct kicked in, and I jumped out my car and draw my gun. I yelled 'Freeze!' to the guy with the shotgun. The perp stopped and turned slowly but fast enough to get a shot off. He looked like he had the devil in his eye with the shotgun pointed right at my midsection. It was him or me as I saw it. Sometimes that's all it takes, a split-second choice.

"I drew down and fired on him, putting two rounds into him, one to the chest and one to the liver. I sat there and watched his eyes dim as he died."

"Was it a clean shoot-out?" the senator asks.

"Turns out he was chasing the very same suspect I'd been on the lookout for all night. The first man I saw running had just raped this man's sixteen-year-old daughter. Caught him right on top of her in the act. Pants down and all, knife to her throat, whole nine yards. And me, trying to be a hero, shot him. A father that was only trying to protect his daughter," I tell the senator as I drift off for a moment, recalling the story of that fateful night. "First time I ever killed a man," I mumble while still in a daze. I believe I black out for a minute, and then I feel the senator's hand on my shoulder, shaking me. I come to and rub my head to clear myself.

"So I left vice squad division to chase murderers with the homicide division, because that's what I felt like. A murderer. All right, so now you know, you can leave now," I say.

"Why do you hate me?" the senator blurts out.

"Just your views, Senator. Your legislation laws and your politics, sir, they don't sit too well with me. I don't hate you, though. I don't know you well enough to hate you," I tell him.

"You're a spiritual man, Garth. Make a connection?"

Then a thought comes to mind of what Terry Ogden at the lottery commission said. "The wickedness in the hearts of men goes way beyond first impressions, Senator."

And right on key, like a child wanting to get in the last word, the senator fires back. "This is your second." Finally, he walks out.

Suddenly, Maxy comes out the kitchen. Surprisingly, he gives a single bark. "What do you think about him? Huh, boy? What you think about him?" I ask my dog. Then Maxy gives another bark. "Yeah, me too." Maxy just breathes quickly. Panting. Then follows up with one more bark.

CHAPTER 14

A few days later I fly to New York City to check out the probate judge that is handling the Caldwell case and to check in on my old partner, Waxton Alvarez. I miss him a lot. We used to have some good times out there ripping and running on vice squad. My flight gets into JFK at ten a.m., and Wax picks me up from the airport. I wave when I spot him and give him a friendly nod as I make my way through the crowded corridor of terminal five. I can see nothing has changed with him. He's crumbling a parking ticket that he has in his hand, which tells me he just got it and probably cursed out the traffic cop who gave it to him. Wax is the type of guy that conceals his detective identity and badge until the very last minute, just to test how far someone else will go on with him.

I walk up to him and give him a hug. I quickly reach for the ticket in his hand. He just laughs and tosses it on the ground.

"How ya been, buddy? Put on a few pounds I see," he jokingly says.

"Ah, you know, more laid back in the South. But look at you," I say. "Losing your hair, Rico Suave, say it ain't so."

Wax starts laughing. "Still banging them, though, G. Every week. The Wax don't change, only the polish," he says. "So what brings you back? Don't tell me you done started something with the locals down there?"

"Since when you known me to be a troublemaker?" I tell Wax a little bit about my Powerball's winner's murder case and let him know I'm doing some follow-ups.

"So how's the captain?" I ask him. Just curious to know how the old boys at the Seventy-Eighth Precinct are doing.

"Cap's fine. He asked about you last week," he tells me. We make a turn in the unmarked black Chevrolet Impala and hit the Grand Central Parkway. As usual with NYC mornings, traffic is crawling and it's slightly raining, which does not help matters. Just for fun, I hit the police siren and the flashing lights on the Impala. Then I pick up the megaphone and start harassing a few brake-loving drivers in front of me. Damn near cause a few accidents. Surprisingly enough, I actually create a moving lane.

Wax quickly grabs the handset from me. "It's only been a year, G," he says.

"Sorry, just had to get this traffic moving," I jokingly tell him. "What tour you on now?"

"Four to twelve," he says. Wax has been on the force for over twenty years. I always tell him to use his seniority but he doesn't. Four to twelve is a shit detail. A lot of domestic violence and robbery calls go down during those hours. Overnight, midnight to eight, was always my shift. Most of the time you're just gathering crime information for the morning crew to follow up on in hopes of making an arrest from the previous night's activity.

"How's Linda and the kids?" I say. When I left New York last year his family was going through a turbulent time. I am hoping things have gotten somewhat better. Linda is a sweetheart who got in way over her head with Wax.

"Linda's Linda," he tells me. "Johnny made the football team, quarterback." How 'bout you?" he asks. "You find a lady down there yet, little side piece to keep your motor running? Your sperm count balanced? Or are you still waiting?" he jokingly says.

"Still waiting," I fire back. He just shakes his head. Wax has been around me for the better half of twenty years. He knows what I've been through with my wife, Allison, passing away ten years ago. It was very hard for me to move on from that. My search for the perfect woman has been difficult. I am always looking for someone that has Allison's standards and qualities, and I just can't find one. She had great virtues that came from being raised as a Christian and being brought up in a two-parent household. She was never one to be running the streets late at night or propping up some rundown bar every weekend. Just a good-natured stay-at-home wife who always made sure I had a meal ready when I came home from work.

"You gotta move on," Wax tells me.

"I'll move on when I'm ready, Wax," I say. I can't expect my old partner to understand my change or my sacrifice. Wax is a different type of monster. Young Spanish lover that is used to women just throwing themselves at him with minimal effort. I'm not sure why he even married Linda. His wife hadn't slept with him for a year after his last stunt of leaving a passed-out hooker in the backseat of the Suburban the morning she needed it to take the kids to school. He simply banged some girl after a night of barhopping with some of his boys at work, then drove home and went to bed. Completely forgot that this drunk chick, probably high on ecstasy, was still passed out in his backseat. When his wife came out with the kids in the morning, the half-naked woman was still sleeping in the back row. She took the kids to school in a cab and left a note on the windshield that read: *I hope the trade-off was worth it.* What a mess that was. I tried to cover

Wax as best as I could on his adulterous whore missions, but I just couldn't get him out of that one.

His wedding had been doomed from the start as well. The night before Wax got married to Linda, me and a couple of cops at vice threw him a bachelor's party. So of course, Wax being the horny Latin toad that he is, he decided to take things a little too far with one of the exotic strippers we hired and went down on her in the middle of the Marriott Marquis hotel floor. And I mean, he was lapping her like a dog. Then he took the stripper, some blonde bimbo, to the back room and banged her. Big surprise, he gave his new wife a venereal disease on their honeymoon night. He blamed the whole thing on his vice squad detail. Sold Linda some story about a few hookers we arrested that spit on us and the like. Linda, being naïve to his ways at that point, bought it. But it never got any better.

"You've been trying to fix things with Linda?" I ask him.

He just shrugs.

"I see there's nothing new under the sun"

"What's that supposed to mean?" he asks.

"You haven't changed," I tell him.

Wax hits the horn at some slow-moving traffic. I can tell I must have struck a nerve with Wax with the talk about Linda. There's a moment of silence in the car during the drive down to the BQE (Brooklyn Queens Expressway) heading toward the Brooklyn Bridge exit in Manhattan.

"Jesus Christ, lady, move it!" he yells out.

"Hey!" I say. "Knock off the blasphemy."

He glares at me. Then we both bust out laughing. That's how it is with us sometimes. We're opposites, but we knew each other's limit. Just to break the ice a little more, I turn on the siren again. Wax immediately turns it off. Then he looks at me. What the hell, I guess he figures, and he turns it back on. We exit off the expressway, lights and sirens blaring.

CHAPTER 15

We arrive at the courthouse on Centre Street right off of Chambers Street, a few blocks from One Police Plaza. When the elevator takes too long, Wax and I take a hike up a few flight of stairs to the fifth floor. I hear Wax wheezing a few steps behind me. He's one cheeseburger away from a heart attack. "Shit, I'm out of breath. Shoulda took the elevator," he says, his hands on his knees. "Who's the judge we going to see again?"

I can't even answer. I'm just as winded as he is. "Probate Judge Lawrence Hastling," I barely blurt out.

"Fucker better be there," he says. We get to room 503B. From the look of things, someone is moving out or just got fired. A few boxes lay about the floor and tacks and nails are clearly visible on a wall where pictures once hung. I see a woman with a folder in her hand just outside the door. She tells me her name is Lisa. I ask her if Judge Hastling is around. Lisa gives me a solemn stare and hangs her head low. I'm taken aback by the look, because in my years in homicide, I'd seen that look one too many times. Then Lisa looks at Wax.

"Were you his brother?" she asks.

As Wax looks at me, I can't help but to get right to the heart of what the hell is going on. "Did you say brother?" I ask.

She nods. "I'm sorry to have to tell you this, but Judge Hastling died last week," she solemnly tells me.

"How?" I almost yell out of frustration.

Then Lisa drops a bombshell on me. "Him and Judge Shumacher were hit by a car while crossing Chambers Street." I jump back in utter shock. Wax can't figure out what just happened. He looks at me.

"Are you kidding me?" I ask, just hoping to hear something else.

"He was on lunch break and a speeding car just came out of nowhere and hit both of them," she says.

"Was it a drunk driver?" I ask.

"Car never stopped. Seemed to be a hit-and-run," she tells me.

Wax grabs my arm, trying to figure out if there's a clear connection between this and my case. He wants to know if I got a break on the case. This is far from it. What we have here is a cold, calculated conspiracy. My client's wife, Jacqueline Caldwell, gets killed by a hit-and-run driver while she's on her way to deposit her first check of her Powerball winnings in Bowling Green, Virginia. Then the lottery commission holds the money until a probate judge decides if the money should continue to the suspected husband, Senator Caldwell. Then on the eve of the ruling concerning the funds, the probate judge who's in charge of that ruling also gets hit by a car. I'd say this is pretty damn far from a break in the case.

I take Lisa into Judge Hastling's office to find out a little bit more about what happened to the judge. Also to see if this is a mere coincidence or if it's directly related to the Caldwell estate. As Lisa wipes the tears from her eyes, she tells me it was lunchtime and in broad daylight. That time of day, the New York City traffic is tight and the streets are extremely crowded. I'm amazed the car had a chance to even get a clear lane. Judge Hastling and Judge Shumacher had just purchased a few hot dogs and sodas when out of nowhere a speeding dark-colored sedan smacked the both of them. As Lisa is telling me the story, I think back to the e-mail I received last week on a random hit-and-run. This was crime sent to me by someone, and at the time I didn't think it was relevant.

I see Wax on the phone down the hall. He immediately started looking into the hit-and-run accident when I told him there might be a connection. Lisa is very distraught over this because she was Judge Hastling's assistant for the last four years. He was an older man, in his late seventies, and his wife is just as old. Lisa tells me she's the one who has to do all the arrangements for his funeral and write the obituary because Judge Hastling hardly had any family.

Wax walks over to us, clearly excited. He explains to me that the 110th Precinct ruled the judge's death a homicide. The four-door sedan had no plates, no tags, and tinted windows. After blurting out all the bad news, he finally gives me something I can look into. There is a bank across the street from the crime scene and a Google street-view camera overhead. *Yes*, I think, *we got the bastard*. However, the footage is downtown at One Police Plaza Precinct, where it's being reviewed. Wax nods to me with excitement. Just like old times.

We were a sharp team together in our days at vice. We once broke a twenty-three-year-old serial killer cold case just on a hunch. Some creep was snatching young girls and cutting them up and placing their body parts all around the Bronx. We had staked out a young streetwalker named Rose because she had similar features to a few victims that had been found in roadside garbage bags. We just figured she could be next based on a pattern we had discovered. "Ring around the Rosie" is what we called the stakeout.

We watched eighteen-year-old Rosie for an entire week. Wax and I lay low in some bushes under the overpass of Hunts Point. We wrote down the make and model and the license plates of every vehicle that passed by for five days. When the right truck came with the right look, and the sketch matched within fifty percent, we moved in. Something about this guy had the right feel, so we stopped him. Lo and behold, it was our guy. Had a body in the backseat and was strolling around looking for another. Case solved. That's how we rolled. A lot of it was just off of gut instinct.

Wax rolls up. "You hot on the senator douche bag for this double homicide, G?" he asks.

"Warm, but not hot," I tell him. I think back to when I'd been in my home talking to the senator, and I remember him telling me that he never contacted the judge over his probate case. He had to know I was going do a follow-up on his story: check all phone records, e-mails, texts, mail correspondence, the whole nine. If the senator lied, I'm going to find out and put the cuffs on him myself.

I walk back over to Lisa, who is pulling out the last few cases that Judge Hastling was working on that year. She spreads them out on the desk and puts them in chronological order according to when the cases appear on the docket. As I flip through the folders I see a bunch of foreclosures, drug seizures, and a few reprocessed storefront properties. I even see a mansion eviction and a freeze on someone's assets, worth about $40 million. Whoa, someone is going to be pissed off about that. Then I see the Caldwell estate folder. I grab it.

"This is it, Lisa," I tell her excitedly.

"The Caldwell estate?" she replies.

"Yes, do you know what the ruling was on this case?"

"Yes, Larry ruled in favor of the deceased lottery woman's husband. He found the husband not liable for his wife's death. We just hadn't sent it in yet."

Wow. I can't make sense of it. If Judge Larry Hastling ruled in favor of the senator getting the money, then why would the senator have had him killed? I'm numb. *Where is this case going?* I think to myself.

"Who came to represent for the husband in court?" I ask Lisa.

"His lawyer, I believe, but I can assure you, no one knew the judge's ruling," she tells me.

"How can you be so sure?" I ask.

"Not unless Larry told someone privately. He knew the husband, Brandon Caldwell." She nods to the estate file. "He and Larry were friends. Caldwell's a senator, you know."

"Yes. Do you think the judge told the senator his ruling?" I ask her.

"It's a conflict of interest to talk to the party under investigation. Larry was way too sharp for that. He would have never jeopardized the case by doing that. Besides, I log every phone call Larry makes," she tells me.

Of course I ask her for the phone log. I can't leave any stone unturned. She tells me the police took it along with a few other items. I prepare to exit the room when Lisa gives me a heartfelt hug, practically begging me to find out who did this. I tell her I will do my best. I give her my card and tell her to give me a call if she should think of anything else that can help me solve this. She nods and puts her head down. I almost get emotional seeing the hurt this death has caused Lisa.

CHAPTER 16

Wax and I head over to the audio/visual department at One Police Plaza to follow up on the video surveillance footage of the hit-and-run. They have an old-school setup with some espionage equipment in the back room of the precinct basement. A small console with a switcher, a few speakers, and six nine-inch television screens against a homemade wooden wall unit. There's an older technician named Joe, who looks to be about sixty-five years old, and a young twenty-something trainee named Rick. Rick keeps telling me there's some new equipment coming soon, and I can tell he's embarrassed to be showing me the footage on these rinky-dink tubes. Nevertheless, it is evidence.

"So what you got?" I ask him.

He shrugs his shoulders. "Not much," he tells me. He runs the one-minute footage, which is distorted and grainy and barely visible.

Out of utter anger over the slow progress of this case I yell out, "You trying to tell me all the cameras in the area of Chambers Street and Broadway are black and white? It's the new millennium, you know."

"That's what I'm trying to tell you," he arrogantly yells back. I look to Wax and toss my hands in the air, wondering where all our tax dollars are going. Even the computers are using old Microsoft software that's in need of an update.

I tell Rick to run the crime footage back but this time slower, at about half the frame rate. He hits a button on the Sony deck and starts to scroll forward with a cylinder knob. From what I can see on the crappy screens, the streets are crowded as usual on a Monday afternoon and there're passersby everywhere. Traffic on Chambers Street going onto the bridge is normal and so is the traffic heading left onto Centre Street, by the courthouses. I pay attention to every vehicle that rolls by. A city bus cruises by followed by a few cars and a messenger bike. Then a horse and carriage creeps in frame with a couple inside who look to be newlyweds. Suddenly, the light turns black, which would be red if this was a color monitor.

"Stop!" I shout. "Now we're sure this is a red light, right?" I ask Rick. Joe the technician hits the pause button and freezes the screen.

"If it was still green, the black-and-white monitor would have been white in this area," Rick says while pointing to the traffic light and circling it with his finger as if I'm a two year old.

I look to Wax and tell him to pay attention to see if we're missing something. I nod to Joe, and he hits play again. A ton of pedestrians stroll across the street on a green light. Then the two judges, Larry Hastling and Jonathan Shumacher, appear, both with hot dogs and sodas in their hands. Coincidentally, a voluptuous woman in a yellow dress grabs their attention. Nothing too extreme, just a slick glance and nods of acknowledgement and approval of beauty from a couple of old-timers. Suddenly, Wax sees something.

"Stop!" he yells to Joe.

Joe immediately hits the pause button. I roll my chair closer to the screen, trying to lock in on Wax's mindset. Rick does the same.

"Do you see the knockers on that babe in the yellow?" he jokingly spurts out. I should have known, seeing who this is coming from. Wax always has his head in the gutter. I kick his chair to snap him back to the seriousness of the matter at hand. "What, she could of been a decoy," he says.

Joe hits the play button again. Surprisingly enough, both judges almost make it to the sidewalk, and I'm talking less than five feet away from the curb. Abruptly, out from the left of the screen, appears a four-door dark-colored sedan. It's at top speed, which is very unusual for that area because of so much pedestrian and commercial traffic.

BOOM! It hits them and only them. You can see on the grainy TV other pedestrians scrambling to get out the way while others run to the judges' aid. I watch as the car skids around the corner but of course I can't get the color, and I'm fifty-fifty on the make and model.

"Looks like a Bonneville or Caprice," Wax blurts out.

"The color, the color! That's what I need. You see where the car went?" I say.

"It's out of frame, but I think it U-turned towards the Brooklyn Bridge. Probably headed to a Staten Island mafia hideaway," Wax indignantly says.

The more I look at the screen, the more I know this was murder. I have no doubt about it. If the judges had been in the front of the pedestrian traffic crossing, maybe I would've given it the shadow of a doubt as an accidental hit-and-run, but they were practically the last ones crossing. Whoever was driving this car waited for them and held the traffic lane clear until it was empty in front of him. He waited until the light was red and then took off. Broadway is the block before and it's almost impossible to take a light there without getting into a car accident. So this car had to be idling just at the corner, waiting for the right moment.

According to the report, they couldn't pull any skid marks because the car never stopped. No tire tread marks from the wheels were left either. It was like a ghost car that came from hell and then disappeared. The way the judges were run over and mangled was just like Jacqueline Caldwell.

I watch the tape a few more times, but I have Joe freeze it each time just before the impact. He can tell it bothers me. After a while I don't have to tell Joe anymore. I am angry. This is pure, unadulterated evil. Judges Hastling and Shumacher were elderly men that shouldn't have died like that. They were at an age probably close to retirement and should've had their final moments on Earth in the privacy of their own homes. Maybe see their grandchildren get married and go to college. They should've died in rocking chairs, sleeping or something. This is horrible.

Wax is to the side, pondering on the case while looking over the report. "Why would the Senator hire you to find the killer, if it's him who's doing the killing, G?"

He has a point, but I have no other suspect. Who else knew the probate judge? Who knew about the lottery winnings? But what really bothers me is no longer *who*, but the *why*. If the probate court gave Senator Caldwell the approval to receive the money, then it has to be someone else that didn't want this to go down. For what reason is what I have to focus on now. Who is to gain, who is to lose, and what is at stake. In my line of work, only two things can cause this type of mayhem: love and money. I have to dig deeper to see if the senator had a disgruntled mistress or if Mrs. Caldwell had a jaded ex-lover. My focus is going to have to shift from the senator to someone new.

CHAPTER 17

I get up and stretch and walk outside. I've been messing with this little piece of coconut that's been stuck in between my teeth all day. It's irritating the hell out of me. I have no toothpick, so I've been making these little paper dart-like airplanes to stick in my mouth to try to get it out. By the time I look down, I have made a mess of the floor. I got the coconut from a donut I ordered at the Dunkin Donuts me and Wax stopped at when I first landed. An apple-filled cinnamon donut and a coconut sugar crème one. I know I can't eat like a teen anymore, but I just had to have one. It was damn good too, but it was way out of line for my health. Down in Virginia, I've stuck with this healthy diet that consists of a lot of vegetables, fruit, and water.

But it's not a myth: cops really do like donuts. I remember in the early nineties when I did a stint on narcotics during the crack era, we would do these weekly drug raids. Before these early-morning door-busting jaunts, we would all gather on the roof of the Pathmark parking garage on 125th Street and Second Avenue in Harlem. A guy named Milo would have three boxes of donuts from Dunkin Donuts or Kripy Kreme set on the roof of one of the unmarked cars. We would dig in like pigs at a slop house. By the time we rolled out, the sugar rush had everyone jumpy. The Narcs would be rocking back and forth, shaking in these tight-ass Chevrolet Impalas. They'd be banging each other in the chest and high-fiving like it was a championship football game and we were getting ready to enter the tunnel.

We would take a door down like the Incredible Hulk and start screaming all sorts of profanities at the suspects. The perps couldn't wait to just get the cuffs on out of fear that they would get killed by one of the sugar-filled hyped-up cops. Most of them would come out in boxer shorts or, on some occasions, even naked. They were just too scared to even move out their beds to grab their pants. It was hilarious, but it would get us by.

Smiling at these memories, I get up and stretch, preparing to walk out of the audio/visual room for a break. "Where you going?" Wax asks.

"Make a call. I miss home," I say while thinking about Sandy and Dominic.

"This is your home," Wax yells back while pointing to a roach on the wall. But it doesn't feel like home anymore. I am done with New York. I haven't been here twelve hours and I am already sick of it. That's what the South can do to you. Once you go out and find there's a whole other world that's slower in pace and a tad bit more connected to human emotion, you tend to fall in love with that place. In my town, everyone speaks to each other like they're related.

I don't feel that sort of connection when I come back to New York City anymore. Everywhere I look there are people on their little gadgets. Whether they are walking across the street, sitting in the parks, or walking their dogs. Everyone is on some sort of mobile device, and from the looks of it, the people of Apple reign supreme. There are iPads and iPhones scattered across the city like a spun web. It is one giant commercial. Steve Jobs lost the battle with cancer, but he sure as hell won the technology war.

I try not to let it get to me too much. It's a short stay here for me in New York. I'm a man on a mission to find out who killed the senator's wife, and why, that's it.

I pull out my phone and start to dial Sandy when Wax taps on the window and waves me in. I come in and there's a breaking news story running on CNN. To my surprise, it's an ongoing active investigation taking place in my town of Caroline County, Virginia. The words *Courtroom Shooting* scroll across the bottom of the screen.

Wax looks away from the screen and glances at me with a raised eyebrow. "Ain't that where you live, G?" he asks.

I'm so focused on what the hell just happened in my city, I don't even answer Wax. "Turn it up!" I yell to Rick. He taps a few bars on the TV remote, but it's still not loud enough. I snatch the remote from Rick and blast it to maximum volume. There's a reporter talking in front of what seems to be the Caroline County Courthouse. Behind him on Main Street are a few emergency service vehicles, fire trucks, and a SWAT truck. Occasionally you can see a Caroline County sheriff's deputy run by toting a shotgun.

The reporter goes on to talk about a courtroom shooting with multiple injuries and possibly some fatalities. The suspect is still at large, and all police personnel are actively pursuing a violent armed and dangerous felon. Then CNN breaks to another reporter with a more recent update. He specifies that two court officers and a stenographer have been shot in the courtroom while proceedings were going on and one of the officers has already succumbed to his wounds. Then the reporter drops a bombshell that leaves me speechless and clutching my chest in pain. He utters the name *Richard Lauson* as the suspect in the shooting. The same son of a bitch that hired me to kill his wife, Sandy, is now a fugitive for two attempted murders and one homicide.

He'd escaped. The sheriff deputies had been moving him from one end of the civil court side of the courthouse to the federal courthouse building when all hell broke loose. While in the back room changing his clothes for the court appearance, Richard had overpowered a correction officer and taken his gun. He'd run into the first courtroom he saw and started shooting like a wild man until he emptied the clip. Then Richard bolted into the street, right through the front door, carjacked a vehicle, and sped off.

This reminds me of the case in Atlanta a few years back with a guy named Brian Nichols, who had escaped custody in an almost identical manner: overpowering a guard and wrestling a gun away from him in the courthouse. He had also killed a few people and eventually surrendered after a Christian woman talked him down. Somehow I can't see that happening with Richard Lauson. He is now a free man who is intent on only one thing, and that is to finish what he started with Sandy. He has nothing else to lose at this point. When he hired me to take out a hit on his wife, he never hesitated to go through with it, even when I tried to talk him down. This guy is cold. Iceman, Richard Kuklinski, cold. There is only one way out for him, and that is death.

Then it hits me—Sandy might not know. As soon as the thought of her name comes to my head, my phone rings. It is Sandy and from the tone of her voice I know I right. She doesn't know. I don't know how to break it to her without scaring her.

"Hi," she says.

"Hey," I reply as I keep one eye on the screen, hoping to see the word *Captured* scroll across. She tells me she just finished putting fresh bandages and ointment on Dominic's scars from the circumcision surgery. I can tell by the sound of her voice that she is happy I picked up. From our last meeting I wasn't too sure how things stood between us.

"I want to apologize for the way I acted when we were in the hospital," she says. "I'm such a mess sometimes."

A load is lifted off of my shoulders. I thought I was the one that freaked her out with my vice squad stories. It bothered me for days, the thought that Sandy was through with me.

"It's fine," I tell her with a sigh of relief. I can hear Dominic in the background moaning and whimpering. He must still be in a lot of pain. In the hospital she told me Dominic was a green belt and third in his class in judo takedowns. I can't imagine him doing any kicking or chopping for a couple of months. "How is he?" I ask Sandy.

"Feeling better. Just like you said, he screamed like hell when he went to the bathroom the first time," she tells me. I chuckle a little. I remember when my mother got me circumcised. I was thirteen years

111

old. I was already into dry-humping girls on my mother's sofa and masturbating to my uncle's porn collection. So being circumcised was a major setback for me at that age. It took months for me to heal and get back to my guilty pleasures.

I ask Sandy how she is feeling. She says she is a little tired and drained but she is thinking it's the medication causing the drowsiness. We chitchat for a few minutes about weather, food, and New York City. Sandy even asks about my dog, Maxy, and who's watching him while I'm out of town. I tell her Maxy is fine. When I leave for small trips my dog is trained well enough to eat sparingly. He knows when I put four or five bowls down in separate locations that I'm going to be gone for just a couple of days. I have an underground tunnel that I built with a latch door that has a hole in the bottom, leads from my basement right into his doghouse in the backyard. Maxy can come and go as he pleases. MaxyIt appears as if Maxy is coming out of his doghouse, but he's really coming from my basement. I got that idea from my stint at narcotics division.

A Dominican drug gang had dug a hole that led from one building to three adjacent buildings in Washington Heights, on 156th Street and Morningside. So when the narcs would raid the building we would always come up empty. Sometimes we would seize the drugs but never get the dealers. Once we got tipped off that there was a tunnel that the dealers were using to get from one end of the block to the other, we seized the entire block. And I'm talking over three hundred people went to get booked at the Seventy-Eighth Precinct just to get four or five suspects. We were fingerprinting mothers, fathers, and grandmothers in the precinct. We didn't give a damn. It was a huge mess, but we had to weed through them all to get to the perps.

My dog's tunnel is nothing too fancy, but a typical burglar couldn't spot it unless he was really searching for an entrance. Only Maxy and I know about the underground tunnel.

While I'm on the phone with Sandy, I can hear her breathing. And that is enough for me. Just knowing there is someone on the other end of the line that is interested in what I have to say is fine.

"You wanna hear something?" she asks me.

"Sure," I tell her. Anything beats hearing these police radios at One Police Plaza all day. I hear her tell Dominic to say what he learned. Then I hear her put the phone on speaker.

"Say hi to Garth," she tells Dominic. I hear Dominic say hi. Then Sandy tells him to do what she told him last night. It's music to my ears as Dominic starts to recite the Lord's Prayer in his baby voice. It brings a huge smile to my face. She actually did what I asked her in the hospital and taught her son Matthew chapter six verses nine to thirteen.

"How long did it take him to learn it?" I ask her.

"Maybe two days." It is beautiful for to me to hear that. As he goes on trying to do the best he can, I can hear Sandy coaching him through it.

"He's a quick learner," I tell Sandy.

"Which way is east?" Sandy asks me.

"Wake up early one morning and wherever you see the sun rising, that's east," I tell her.

She tells me that when I left the hospital she started to read the Bible that was on the table. I tell her I'm going to bring her a King James Version back from New York for her to read. Then it happens again, another moment of silence. Just breathing and background noise.

"I see that selfishness you had about you is changing," I tell her.

"Only certain people can bring the best out of me, I guess," she replies. Then there's silence again for a space of about thirty seconds. In the silence my mind has a chance to think. I have to keep reminding myself that this is a business acquaintance and still a married woman. I look for an out before my inner thoughts concerning Sandy get the best of me.

"All right," I say. "I'm glad you and the boy are both doing well. I'll ring you when I get back in town."

"You won't be running for long," she fires back.

"Excuse me?" I say.

Sandy tells me how she filed for divorce a few days ago and the lawyer is drawing up the papers for her husband to sign. So telling me I won't be running for long is a jab at me about running from her because she's married. I don't really respond to it. It's clear she hasn't turned on the TV yet because if she had she would have seen breaking news about her husband on every channel.

"Just hurry home," she says.

"Sandy, I want you to stay at my house until I get back."

"Your house?" she asks.

"Yes, something has happened and you're not safe. Richard...your husband...um, he escaped about an hour ago and shot a few people in the process. Chances are he's gonna come looking for you. I have a key in my flowerpot at the entrance of my door, under the lilies. Grab a few things for you and Dominic and stay at my house until Richard is captured. Please," I compel her.

Sandy is speechless. I'm pretty sure this has hit her hard. "Okay, Garth, I will," she calmly says. Then just like that she hangs up. I plop down in my chair. Wax comes over.

"What's up?" he asks.

"Remember that woman in Virginia on the hit-for-hire case I told you about?"

"Yeah," Wax says.

"Yeah, well, my business relationship with the intended victim has somewhat evolved and taken a turn for the heart, and guess who this is on CNN?"

"The husband that hired you to kill her."

"Yep," I reply.

"My friend, you do have problems. Maybe you should head back. Let me finish the follow-up on this thing," he consolingly says.

"Maybe you're right." Me and Wax head out.

CHAPTER 18

We stop on Fifth Avenue at FAO Schwartz toy store. I want to pick up a few items for Dominic, including a furry stuffed dog that resembles Maxy, seeing that they are going to be staying with me. The woman hands me my receipt and we take off. Inside the police car, Wax gets a little curious about the items I purchased and starts asking questions.

"So are you actually dating this woman yet?" Wax blurts out.

"No, but I'm having a hard time being around her," I say while putting my head down in shame.

"Don't tell me..." Wax replies. But I beat him to the punch.

"I didn't touch her."

"But you want to?" he asks.

"Yes," I say.

"Ha! You sinner. I knew you was faking," he fires back at me. I have to laugh. It's funny when people see you try to get your life together and get all the impurities out of your system, how they can't wait to see you fall. It's almost like it gives them a sense of dignity about themselves. Like it makes their faults more valid because someone else has slipped. I never understood that.

"Hey, asshole, that's why I didn't touch her. Her idiotic husband that hired me to kill her was in the process of getting served divorce papers," I angrily tell him.

But Wax, as usual, can't understand it. "Well, what are you waiting for, G? He's a fugitive. He's done. You might as well start tapping it now."

I try to explain to Wax from a spiritual perspective. "Adultery is a serious crime to God, Wax. It has to be done in order. That's what I'm most comfortable with."

Wax doesn't respond. He just looks at me and gives me a tap on the shoulder. Almost as if he is relieved to hear I am keeping it real with my faith. I can tell he misses me. He gets on me about not e-mailing him and calling him enough since I left New York. I take a shot at trying to bring Wax to the light by offering him my Bible. He jokingly throws up cross with his fingers and hisses like a vampire does when he sees a cross. He eventually takes the Bible and puts it in the glove compartment. I'm hoping one day he will use it.

"I love you, man," he tells me while rubbing the top of my head, messing up what little hair I have left. "Can I ask you a serious question?"

Uh-oh, I think to myself, *here he comes with one of these left-field questions that stirs more strife than gives answers.* "Sure, go ahead, anything," I tell him.

"That night on Second Avenue, with the shooting of the lesbian, was that really an accident?"

It's funny how he's bringing that up seeing as I just recited that same story to Sandy in the hospital just a few days before. "Truthfully, I don't know what got into to me that night," I tell Wax. "I wasn't really under my own control. I can't explain it, but half of me didn't want to shoot her and the other half did. One of my halves took over and won that night, Wax," I say.

"So what you are saying is that the devil made you do it?"

"No, what I'm saying is that there's a force even higher than the devil. The devil has to answer to someone too, you know."

Wax comes back again. "The only force that is higher than the devil is…"

"God," I say. Then I turn to Wax with a blank expression on my face. I see him pondering my answer for a while as we drive through the city. Then out of the corner of my eye I see him nod slightly to himself. I think he finally gets it. He turns to me in amazement.

"God," he says. "I believe you, brother, I believe you." Wax comes to a sudden halt in front of a bodega in the Lower East Side.

"Where you going, Wax? I gotta flight to catch," I say.

"Let me just play my lotto and evening Win-4. It's seventy-five million dollars this week. I got a few minutes," he says while hustling into the store. I shake my head. Just thinking about the lotto immediately puts me back on the Jaqueline Caldwell Powerball case. Here we go.

CHAPTER 19

I'm back in Virginia and it's warm and sunny, and traffic is flowing just great. I feel at home already. I take a drive over to the Tenth Precinct to do some follow-ups. New York wasn't a complete dead end for me, but I didn't get the answers I was looking for. So I'm going to tap back into the source of the investigation. Plus, thinking about Sandy, Dominic, and Richard still being out there made me come back a day earlier than I planned.

I go to see a Detective Panoli Spazolli to talk to him about Jacqueline's hit-and-run case. Last time I was there, Detective Panoli was on vacation, so I didn't get to hear his side of the story on the way things went down with the search for the suspect or suspects. He was the lead investigating officer in charge of the Caldwell case. He also might hold the missing pieces of the puzzle facing me. Maybe even a few new leads or something.

On my way to see Panoli, Detective Fuller and another detective, Joe Johnson, hold up a newspaper for me to see. "Your suspect escaped, Colombo," Fuller jokingly yells.

"Yeah, P.I.," Johnson joins in. "Fucker killed a court officer, too. Why don't you drop everything and help us nab this bastard?"

I don't entertain the dialogue. I reach in my pocket and pull out the lottery ticket that Detective Fuller had given me a few weeks earlier. I walk over to him and put the ticket on his desk. "No luck," I tell him.

"I thought you skipped town with my winning ticket," he says back.

"Wow, last week I was benevolent and you liked my demeanor, this week I'm a thief," I fire back while taking a bag of chips off his desk. "Spazolli back from vacation yet?" I ask Fuller. He nods to the back room of the precinct. I walk over to Spazolli's office and lightly knock on the door.

"Enter," a voice screams through the door. I walk into the office and quickly scan the place to determine the type of man I'm dealing with. You can tell a lot about a cop when you see how organized or messy his place of work is. From what I see, Detective Panoli Spazolli is an unorganized police officer. There are scattered folders and guns and ammo magazines everywhere. An open box of donuts and a few empty coffee cups in an overflowing waste basket. At first glance I think I see a roach running behind a picture on the wall. There's even a lingering odor in the room. Panoli has a six-foot picture window behind his head that is closed as if he likes the smell in his stuffy office. The shades are drawn, allowing just a trickle of sunlight into the dim interior.

I immediately start talking to Spazolli about the case and what I've been up to on my end. He says he was hot from the get-go for the senator regarding the murder of Jacqueline, just as I was in the beginning, but the senator had an airtight alibi. Plus, from all the running around and research I've done, I am ready to rule the senator out as a suspect completely.

Spazolli asks me about the surveillance footage from New York. I tell him it wasn't very fruitful. The car hit both judges and turned onto the bridge and that was it. Plus, we still don't have the color of the vehicle. I am surprised to learn that one of the tapes from a nearby bank was stolen the same day the judges were killed. Could that be a coincidence? I wonder. When I dig deeper about the stolen tape, I am shocked to learn that the bank had an overnight break-in and all the audio/video equipment was destroyed. All the news isn't bad, though. Panoli tells me that they do have a few witnesses who stated that it was a burgundy four-dour sedan, possibly a Nissan Maxima, that hit the judges. That's a breakthrough. I start to get a little excited about the new information when all of a sudden it hits me. These guys dropped the case and put it off as a hit-and-run. Even after all the evidence pointed to foul play.

"Why did you drop the case?" I curiously ask.

"It wasn't dropped, it was pushed back," Spazolli tells me. "I had already been on this thing for six months. We weren't coming up with any new leads and new murder cases just kept piling up, if you know what I mean," he says while tapping on the two-foot-tall pile of files.

"Not vehicular homicides, I hope?" I jokingly say.

Spazolli doesn't laugh. He almost seems like he doesn't want to talk about the case, judging from his demeanor. Sometimes as a private detective, you don't get the respect of real cops, so to speak. But the one thing that makes this unit at the Tenth Precinct a little uncomfortable with me is that I was a real cop before I became a private eye. Not only a real cop but a cop out of big-time New York City's homicide and vice squad divisions. I've always felt they were a little intimidated by my presence, or maybe even jealous. But even with knowledge and wisdom I gained while policing in the Big Apple, I've kept myself humble with the squad. I never throw around my status as a supercop or my weight as a narcotics/vice cop in the big city. I just stay in my place as a private investigator and try not to get in the Virginian guys' way or stand them up. They are nice enough to let me tag along with them on some of their cases and throw me a bone when I need help. But with this case I have to push a little harder. I tell Spazolli something he might not like to hear.

"Well, it's time to reopen the Caldwell case, there's been another murder."

He bangs his hand on the desk, causing a few folders to topple over. "Here, related to this case? I don't think so," he angrily says.

My immediate thought is to wonder why Spazolli would be so surprised about the news. They did a half-assed job on the investigation. With me traveling to different states and pulling up all sorts of coincidental evidence, they should have known I was going to find something.

"Yeah," I say with a tenacity to match his fist bang.

I see Spazolli shaking his head in denial as he looks at his watch like he has somewhere to be. I'm thinking, *Lazyass Virginia police department just looking for a way out because they don't want to do the work.*

"That's a little out of my jurisdiction, Garth. But as a private eye, I'm sure you have all the time in the world to investigate vehicular homicides in New York and any other state. I, on the other hand, am dealing with a new wave of drug-related murders. Ugly ones. In case you haven't heard, the Mexican cartels have found a new safe haven to do their business, and it's turning our once peaceful, beautiful city streets red with blood," he indignantly says as he picks up four folders from the desk and slams them in front of me.

"And on top of that," he continues, "your hit-for-hire perpetrator, that asshole husband, just made a violent escape from custody. We're sort of tied up on that, too. So feel free to look through the files if you want to help your case, but they're not to leave this office. I have to log all this stuff in at the end of the year," he angrily says.

I understand where Spazolli's tension is coming from. As a former cop, I have to put myself in his shoes. Many days at the Seventy-Eighth Precinct in Brooklyn, we were bogged down with murders, rapes, and robberies. Only priority felonies got pushed to the forefront. If it was a case with high-profile media attention, you could forget anything else. It's just the way it goes sometimes in crime-fighting. Besides, I am the one that brought Richard Lauson into this small-town Virginia police station, so the guys feel I should take a tad bit of responsibility for the path of destruction he blazed in his escape.

Also, on the front page of the morning's *Northern Virginia Daily* was a headline that read: *Headless Horsemen*. The police found eight headless bodies of young Mexican men in a burned-out minivan in the parking lot of a Sonic Drive-In restaurant. Why the Mexican gangs and the cartel affiliates are moving into this part of the country, I can't tell you. All I know is there's been a spike in gun-related homicides in the last seven months. And now this wave of cartel violence is something out of a horror movie. Kidnappings, drive-by shooting, hanged body parts with missing limbs are becoming a daily occurrence. The Virginia PD is not ready for this.

"Spazolli, I'm not trying to tell you how to do your job. It's just that a woman who was supposed to come into a lot of money and live her life rich and prosperous, with her husband, who might've been the forty-fifth president of the United States, had her dreams suddenly cut short. And whoever killed her is still out there, cutting other lives short. Nothing bothers you about that?" I ask him.

"Besides the possibility of a senator's involvement, no," he says. "Homicide is an everyday occurrence in the world, Garth. She was just a victim of the circumstances."

I am in shock at that statement coming from a veteran cop. Virginia or not, Spazolli is still a police officer, and it seems that this job has finally desensitized him. I can't even respond. I just glare at him with mixed feelings of vehemence and pity. Then, just for the sake of a cheap shot, I throw a little jab his way.

"How was Spain?" I nonchalantly ask.

"Who?" he replies.

"Never mind," I say as I walk out of his office and slam the door behind me, leaving him and the stink locked in.

CHAPTER 20

I go back home and shift my focus to some paperwork that I snatched from Spazolli's office when he wasn't looking. I want to see if I can pick up some sort of trail in all this mess. I am lying on my bed, looking over the files. As usual, Maxy is lying next to me tearing at an artificial bone I brought him back from New York. I have a half-filled glass of Chardonnay on my night table and ESPN on the tube. Back home, in New York, there is talk of a guard named Jeremy Lin who is bringing the New York Knicks back to their former greatness.

Sitting in my living room are Sandy and Dominic. She took my advice and came over after finally seeing the news of her husband's escape. She said she wouldn't get in my way when I told her I had to work. I even offered her and Dominic the bedroom for more privacy, but she refused. Though she is appreciative of my concern and protectiveness, Sandy doesn't want to become a burden on me like some sort of helpless woman in despair. She told me she'd take care of their own meals just as long as she didn't have to go back home until Richard was arrested. So I obliged her request and gave her what she needed.

Dominic isn't one of those hyperactive ADHD kids that have been popping out of the woodwork in the last decade. He is a calm kid that is somewhat of a mama's boy but not a crybaby. I like that about him. Even after the circumcision, he didn't seem to whine and moan as a ploy to get his mother's attention. I watch him in the living room through the crack in my bedroom door as he plays with my miniature basketball and messes around with my home computer.

Sandy is chomping on some grapes and watching one of the housewives shows on the flat screen. I've never understood women who get hooked on these train-wreck shows about dysfunctional families. At times, these housewives shows can be entertaining, but they are all disasters waiting to happen. Sometimes you hear of the participants committing suicide after the first season, but America still loves them.

As I flip through the files and the evidence, I can't understand how Spazolli and the boys at the Tenth Precinct didn't conclude that this was cold-blooded murder. Spazolli, who was lead investigator on the Caldwell case, is so wrapped up in other murder cases that he didn't even flinch when I told him another murder related to Jacqueline's death has been committed. When I mentioned it to him, I was a little thrown off that he figured it was vehicular homicide.

In the files, I find out that the late Jacqueline Caldwell had a newly bought wedding ring on her finger. The net worth for this rock of a diamond was $32,000. Along with that, another marriage was being planned for the senator and Jacqueline. It was going to be sort of renewal of vows to be held at Dartmouth's trendy estate in two months. Does that sound like a husband who wanted to kill his wife?

Also, that month they made three trips to the gynecologist. It seems Jacqueline, who was in her early forties, was going to be a mother for the first time. I can't believe it. The senator, who is a staunch advocate of pro-choice abortion, was going to have a child. Would he have gone as far as killing his wife to avoid having kids? You better believe I am going to ask him.

As I'm looking at the medical report on how far along Jacqueline was with her pregnancy my phone rings. Maxy jumps up and starts going crazy and knocks over my wine with his tail. This is a little unusual for Maxy, because he hardly barks at the phone ringing at all. By now Dominic and Sandy have gotten up and come into the room to see what's gotten into my dog. The phone rings again and Maxy is still at it. I can see Dominic cowering behind his mother, holding onto the furry stuffed animal I brought him. Maxy is now mixing in a little growling with his loud bark.

"Shut up, Maxy!" I yell to him.

"What's wrong with him?" Sandy asks.

"Not sure, I've never seen him act like this for a phone ring before," I say. Finally, I pick up the phone just to get him to shut up. I usually don't answer the phone when I'm working, but this is an exception. "Garth Henderson," I say into the phone.

It's none other than Senator Brandon Caldwell causing the disturbance. He hears Maxy barking in the background. "Must've known it was me calling," he jokingly says.

I respectfully tell the senator that I'm working and I have company. He's all bent out of shape because I didn't come by his house this weekend like I promised. I can hear it in his tone. What the senator doesn't know is how busy I've been on this case.

"I've been calling your place all week," he says.

"I was out of town, Senator," I fire back. While I have the senator on the phone, I throw him a few questions to clear my conscious about his whereabouts for the week just to see if he was in New York. He gets a little aggravated at my line of questioning and demands that I come by his house tonight. It gets my curiosity going as to what the senator could have that he wants me to see so badly. I let the Senator know I'll be there in about an hour and that I am going to walk Maxy first, but he insists that I come right now and bring my dog with me if need be.

I hang up and grab the dog collar and leash off the table. I tell Sandy I'm going to walk Maxy and I'll be back. Suddenly, the phone rings again. I figure it's the senator calling back to tell me to hurry up, but I'm note 100 percent sure. It rings a few times, and this time Maxy surprisingly doesn't bark.

I answer and it's Lisa, Judge Hastling's assistant from New York. She is calling to give me a few numbers that were logged in as the judge's last calls to his office phone. I don't have time to chat, so I give her my e-mail address and tell her to send the numbers that way. It's thoughtful of her to follow up on the call log. I remember how distraught she was over the judge's death, so I know this must be important. I thank Lisa and tell her I'll keep her posted on the investigation.

Sandy can tell by the smoothness of my voice that I am talking to a woman on the other line. I think I even see a touch of jealousy in her face when I hang up the phone.

"You want company?" she asks, as I get ready to take Maxy with me to the senator's house.

"With this guy I'm about to meet, I might be a while, Sandy" I tell her. "You and Dominic can just relax here tonight. I'll be back later on." I find myself fighting to pull Maxy out the door, as he seems hesitant to leave.

The weather is pretty cool in Caroline County tonight. The streetlights and a full moon cast a beautiful mix of evening light. As I walk down the empty street with Maxy, there's a stillness in the air to the point of being eerie. I can hear other dogs barking in the distance, but that's it. Then, suddenly, even the barking stops. It almost feels like Maxy and I are the only living things in the whole of Central Point, Virginia.

Then Maxy gives one bark and riles up a whole slew of barking dogs in the surrounding blocks. Must be some sort of code they have. Then, just like that, all goes mute again. I let go of the leash and put it in Maxy's mouth as he walks alongside me. My dog has been disciplined like that from when he was a puppy. He never leaves my side.

I take a look around because I'm having a strange feeling that I'm being watched. It could be because I'm about to go to a senator's house on a murder investigation or it could be that Richard hasn't yet been caught. Either way, I'm feeling a little paranoid tonight.

I grab the chain out of Maxy's mouth and start to head to my car, looking both ways before crossing the street. Maxy enters the street first. Then, just as I'm about to follow him, a speeding vehicle comes out of nowhere, flying over a grassy field across the street from me. At first glance I can tell it's a dark-colored sedan with no lights and it's heading straight toward me. I quickly run and jump back on the sidewalk. I try to pull Maxy with me, but the force of the jump pops the cheap leash right off of his neck.

By now the car is right on top of us, and I scream to my dog, "Maxy, run!" as I reach for my firearm. But it's too late. Maxy takes the full impact of the front grill and goes airborne into a concrete wall. I immediately draw down and start firing my .38 revolver at the vehicle. This is a downgrade from my sixteen-shot 9mm Glock I was used to carrying in New York. I just figured as a private investigator in Virginia, my days of having to unload a full magazine on a perp were over.

Just to be frugal with my hollow-point bullets, I take my time with the last three shots and follow the vehicle as it speeds down the street. I inhale and calmly take the last three shots, hoping to at least score one hit in a shoulder or something. I manage to shatter the back windshield and take out a tire. I can tell by the burst of smoke and the flash that ignites in the night air that the driver is now running on the wheel's rim.

To my surprise, after the sixth shot, the car comes to a complete screeching halt. Suddenly, I see brake lights, then white lights, and the vehicle starts to reverse. Oh shit, he knows I'm out. I reach for my speed-loader rounds for my .38 and realize I have nothing. I was just going for a quick walk then I was going to throw Maxy in the backseat and head over to the senator's house. Why would I be carrying extra rounds?

As I look at the car backing up, I suddenly see flashes from a gun muzzle flaring out of the shattered rear window. If you're curious about light being faster than sound, I can tell you: yes, it is. The driver fires a full magazine my way, and this time it is an automatic weapon.

I roll. I jump. I tumble. I do anything I can to get out the way of those bullets. I manage to make my way over to a neighbor's house and jump in some bushes. I can hear the bullets whizzing past me and hitting the bushes. After a few seconds, the shooting stops, and I hear the car peel out. I take a look and see a cloud of smoke lingering, like you see in cartoons.

I slowly creep out from the bushes with my head bleeding from the fall and a stinging sensation in my right shoulder. My adrenaline is ramped up to a thousand as I run over to Maxy.

"Maxy," I say. No response as I pick him up. I can see his lower ribs protruding through his fur. He's breathing real heavy and there's a slight wheezing noise coming out of his mouth. "Hold on, baby," I say to him.

I run back home and put Maxy in the front seat of my car. By now Sandy and Dominic are outside on my lawn. They must've heard all the commotion. I try to jump in the car without getting Sandy or her son involved, but she's not having any of it.

"Was that Richard?" she says with fear in her voice.

"Not sure," I reply.

She runs over to the driver's side. "Move over, I'll take you to the hospital," she says while putting Dominic in the backseat.

"I'm not going to the hospital. I need to find a veterinarian quick. Maxy's been hit by a car!" I yell back at her. I'm still pumped up with adrenaline and pure anger.

"You've been shot, Garth. You need a hospital," she says with even more tenacity.

Just then I feel the stinging sensation again in my shoulder and arm. I finally look down, and lo and behold, there's a bullet hole. It's a through-and-through hole the size of a dime, and it's leaking a lot of blood. That fucker shot me. But I look back at Maxy and the ol' boy's wheezing is getting louder, and a slight, faint whimper noise is starting up.

"I'm fine. I need a vet hospital now, Sandy. I'll go to the hospital after I get Maxy checked in."

Sandy pulls out her iPhone and types in a quick search. She puts Dominic in the back seat, then jumps in the driver's side seat. "There's one fifteen miles away. I'll drive," she tells me. Then she peels out.

CHAPTER 21

A few minutes later we arrive at the veterinarian. I jump out and grab Maxy and run through the doors, screaming, "My dog's been hit, my dog's been hit!"

A small staff of vet doctors comes running over to Maxy, and I can see by the look in one of the intern's faces that this is bad. Some of the employees that work at these animal shelters and veterinarian hospitals are high school students and college kids who just love animals. So it's always hard on them when they see an abused or hurt animal.

I notice one of the vets looking at me as I pass Maxy to them. Then I realize my whole shirt is drenched in blood. With all the drama surrounding Maxy, I had forgotten that I'd been shot.

"Are you all right, sir?" one of the ladies asks me.

"I've been shot, but I'm okay," I tell her.

"We can treat that here until an ambulance gets here if you want."

"No, I'm fine."

"Sir, you can go into hypovolemic shock. Let me just get you something," she says, practically begging me to allow her to help. Sandy gives me a nod of approval as well.

I walk over to a room while Maxy is carried to another. I hear one of the interns on the phone with 911 while the vet I'm with is cutting off my shirt to see the hole. She cleans it up with some gauze, peroxide, and alcohol. She hands me two eight-hundred-milligram pain pills and sprays some solution that numbs my arm. My bleeding has slowed down by now.

With all this going on, a thought rushes to my head that this could've been the senator trying to set me up. He's the only one who knew I was leaving my house at that moment. It could have also been Richard, who found out where I live. I'm not too sure which way to lean at the moment. And since I can't rule out any of them as suspects, I go with the sure thing that I can rule in or out.

I tell Sandy to stay with Maxy and I'll be back. I jump in my car and grab a shirt from the trunk, and I hightail it over to Senator Caldwell's house. I am on edge because somebody tried to kill me tonight. My guess is I'm getting too close to the truth and this killer doesn't want to be exposed.

Running through the events of the last hour in my head, I remember the driver's knowing to stop after I fired all six of my shots. The only people I know that count live rounds are professionals. Then right after that, sixteen shots came whizzing back at me from what sounded like a Glock 17. I could hear them blazing past my head, making this whistling sound. By the grace of God, only one bullet hit me, and the damage is not life threatening.

I arrive at the senator's house with one intention, and that is to get answers. What would Sam Spade do? crosses my mind. I get up to the senator's door fully drenched in sweat. The medicine I took at the animal clinic along with my adrenaline has my heart rate sky-high. I bang on the senator's door. I give it no more than two seconds before I bang again. I even throw a steel-toed kick in there.

Finally, the senator answers the door, sporting a Tommy Hilfiger robe with matching red slippers. I waste no time with the Senator, immediately pulling out my revolver and putting it to his neck. I use my other hand to take hold of the senator's robe. Even though I know the gun is empty, I still have to bluff.

"Open the garage, now!" I grunt at the senator. He is shocked at my actions, and he tries to pull back. I tighten my grip on his robe, almost crushing his chest as I squeeze with every ounce of my remaining strength.

"What are you, crazy? What's wrong with you? You're a cop," he says in one single breath.

At this point I don't want to hear anything. I need proof. "The garage, Senator!" I say with fury in my eyes and venom in my voice.

"What's this about, Garth? I called you, remember?" he says. "Garth, my neck."

I push the gun deep into the senator's neck to the point that I can feel his esophagus.

"All right, all right!" he squeals. I walk the senator inside where he grabs his keys with the garage remote on them off the table. I lead the senator through the back door to the rear of his house. The senator presses a button on his key chain, causing the garage to rise. I step away, grabbing the senator with me, because I'm expecting anything or anyone to jump out at this point. My alert senses are on a New York high.

"Don't move," I tell the senator as I go over to the hoods of the cars and start feeling them. Damn, all cold. They aren't even the same make and model of the car in question. He has a Mercedes 500SL coupe and a silver Range Rover in the front of the garage. He also has an older model Rolls-Royce buried deep in the back. Outside, in front, he has the bulletproof, satellite-equipped Cadillac Escalade ESV that his driver uses to move the senator around in. I look around his three-car garage for any sign of a Chevrolet Impala, Nissan Maxima, something. Anything to tie the Senator to the attempt on my life would be great.

"What are you looking for? the senator says.

"Where is it?" I yell back while still scanning the garage. Finally, I ease up. It wasn't him. I ease my trigger back on my empty .38 and pocket it.

"You mind telling me what the hell is going on?" he asks.

"Somebody just tried to kill me and Maxy," I tell him.

"Who? How? You all right?" *All good questions*, I think to myself.

We both go inside the house. The senator pours me a glass of wine to ease the tension.

"I don't see how you could of figured me for this, Garth. I'm trying to get to the bottom of this murder just like you. I hired you, so why would I try to kill you?" the Senator says while taking a full gulp of his wine.

"I don't trust anyone at this point, Senator. Do you know Judge Lawrence Hastling was killed last week?" I tell him.

"Oh my God, Larry. He's dead?"

"Yes, he is. So I'm gonna ask you some questions and honest answers would be very helpful right now for everyone," I say to the grieving senator.

"How was he killed?" the senator asks.

"Hit-and-run," I tell him. The senator sighs. He knows this murder is somehow related to his wife's case. There's an uncomfortable moment of silence in the room. Then the senator looks at my shoulder, which has started leaking blood again.

"Do you need another bandage for that, or another shirt?" he asks.

"No," I angrily say. "I need to know why you didn't go with your wife to deposit the check. We're talking five million dollars, Senator," I say.

The senator shakes his head in disappointment. "She just couldn't wait. All that week I was dealing with a new crime bill. Some fifteen-year-old kid jacked a woman for her car and accidentally killed her infant son in the backseat when she pushed the gun out of her face. The state wants to drop the age of adult charges to thirteen," he tells me.

"Thirteen? That's just a baby."

"A baby until it's your mother on the pavement, Garth."

I start to go into the senator's personal life. "Do you have an ex-wife, a mistress, some disgruntled political foe maybe? A right-wing stalker from your sick, twisted tribe of politicians?" I ask.

The senator gets up and walks into the dining room. Comes back with a DVD. He pops it in the DVD player. We sit there and watch a clip of his wife getting hit by the car. I am only able to rewind it once before I know the senator can't take it anymore. When I look to the side, the senator is wiping his tears. I am sort of shaken up myself. Not every day you get to see your wife murdered on video.

"I'm sorry, Senator. If you don't mind me asking, why did you steal the tape?" I calmly ask him.

"Do I look like a thief?" the senator says. "This was sent to me."

I am shocked. There are some cold-blooded people in the world, but this is taunting at an all-time high. Who would send this tape to the family of the victim? What heartless soul would do such a thing?

I remember reading up on the Cheshire, Connecticut home invasion murders of the Petite family in 2007 by those two creeps, Steven Hayes and Joshua Komisarjevsky. It wasn't enough that these two demons raped and killed the mother and her two daughters. The fuckers had to go and burn up the house to try to conceal the evidence. But those two bastards went as far as writing taunting letters from prison to the surviving father, William Petite, who they had bludgeoned with a baseball bat and bound up in the basement, calling him a wuss for not protecting his family. Saying he could've gotten free and stopped it but he was too scared. Spewing all sorts of hate and blame on the surviving victim for not doing enough to save his family. Imagine how William felt reading those letters, especially after hearing his wife, Jennifer, and his two daughters, Hayley and Michaela, screaming out their burning lungs to their last breaths. I'm sure it will haunt him forever. Needless to say, those two demons both got the death penalty, but the psychological damage from the letters and possibly believing he could've done something more will torment William for years.

The senator goes back into the living room and comes back out with a manila envelope. He hands it to me with a distressed look on his face. It contains a letter inside with a note attached to the front that reads: NO MORE SHALL YOU DESTROY OUR FUTURE. I pull out the letter and hold it up next to the overhead dining room light to look for smudge prints, hair, or rug fibers. Anything to get a DNA hit would help. Of course, it's clean as a whistle.

"Why didn't you turn this in to the local authorities?" I ask the senator.

He sort of shrugs it off nonchalantly. "I didn't trust anyone. I was scared. They sent it to me a week after Jackie was murdered. They could have just killed me, Garth. Why not just kill me? Why not me?" the senator solemnly says. Suddenly, he starts crying hysterically. And I mean uncontrollably bawling mixed in with lowpitch moans and a cat sound. It is piercing my ears to hear a man go on like that.

I try to console him with a hug and a pat on the back until I realize I am smearing blood all over his Tommy Hilfiger robe. I speak some words from the spiritual side of things, trying to give the senator a different view of this hardship he is going through.

"God works in mysterious ways, Senator. Ways we sometimes can't understand. We just have to learn to except the losses and rejoice with the gains. Consider Job and what he went through," I tell him.

"You ever lose something close to you?" the senator asks.

"I too lost my wife, sir. She died ten years ago on the operating table while giving birth to my daughter. Then she died as well a few hours later," I tell him.

Suddenly my phone rings, and it's Sandy on the line. She tells me the worst news a man can hear. Maxy is gone. The wounds were just too much for the doctors to fix. I got Maxy when he was just a puppy. I can remember the first day I got him from a relative of mine. I had him sleep in the room with me on his own dog bed. It even had a pillow and blanket just like mine. He would walk with me everywhere. I tell Sandy that I'll be home late but she should go back to my house and lock all the doors.

Now I am really upset. This killer has taken something precious and loved from both of us—the senator and me—and he's going to pay for it with his life.

"My dog died tonight," I tell the senator. He looks at me with pity in his eyes. He knew I loved my dog.

"What are we gonna do about this, Garth? Should I call the feds?" he asks.

"No. I'm gonna finish this myself," I tell him. We plop down on the sectional sofa, both of us deep in thought. Trying to figure this thing out. I ask the senator a few more questions about his life. His past. His future. Just trying to get an angle on who might want to get at him. I look at the letter and read it a few times and come up with nothing but a hate-filled article that reads like someone's journal.

As I look around the room at the pictures all over the senator's wall, one particular photo catches my eye. I get up and move closer. It is a photo of what appears to be a young senator and three friends in an auditorium. The woman on the left looks very familiar, as if I've met her somewhere before.

"Who's this woman?" I ask as I point to the woman with reddish-brown hair. The senator gets up and walks over to the picture. He looks at the woman and gives a small grunt.

"That was my high school sweetheart," he says.

"Her name?"

"Terethia, why?" he asks.

As I'm looking at this picture, I'm racking my brain to try to remember where I've met her before. "She looks so familiar. Do you have a better picture of her, something more recent?"

The senator goes in a draw under his mirror and pulls out a few albums. Most of them are from his childhood years and family outings. Then he pulls out his high school yearbook from Andrew Jackson High School in Saint Albans, Queens, 1977. He takes a few swipes at the cover to try to clear some of the dust off of it. He opens it and flips a few pages.

"Here," he tells me. "We were an item all four years at Jackson."

I grab the book and take a deep look at this young girl. I zoom in on the face and focus mainly on the eyes. Then I see it. But before I say anything, I ask the senator for a pencil. He gives me one, and I start to color in the woman's hair from reddish brown to jet black.

"Terry fucking Ogden," I inadvertently blurt out loud, looking back up at the picture on the wall.

"Who?" the senator asks.

"Senator, this woman was your high school sweetheart?" I ask him again.

"Yes, why? You know her?" he replies.

At first I am afraid to even tell the senator. But the picture I am looking at of a young Brandon Caldwell before he was a politician, posing with a young redhead girl who was Terethia Ogden before she became the head of securities at the Multi-State Lottery Association, clearly shows the woman I met just a few days ago. This is a bombshell of major proportions being dropped. My heart starts pounding in my chest. I don't even feel the bullet wound in my shoulder anymore. On the bottom of the picture is a circled slogan that reads: *Couple of the year*. I can't hold it in anymore.

"Mr. Senator, you're not going to believe this, but I met this woman a few days ago in Iowa. She is the head of the securities and integrity department of the Multi-State Lottery Association. She's a brunette now, did you know that?" I ask him.

"Really? You said you saw her in Iowa? What were you doing out there? How did you meet her, of all people?" he says, all in that one-breath questionnaire style he has.

I explain to the senator that I'd gone up to Iowa to do research on his case and on the Powerball game itself. Being that she is the head of the securities firm that deals with distributing the winnings to the clients, she has to know who he is. Her department has to do extensive research on every winner, especially a Powerball winner with a $110 million jackpot.

I told him that Terethia is on the lottery association board in West Des Moines, Iowa, and when I spoke to her she acted like she didn't even know him. The senator is in complete denial. He tells me that there is no way Terethia would not have remembered him. Especially after going through so much together during their relationship. So I press him for details.

After a few more glasses of wine, the senator tells me a story about his tumultuous, four-year-long relationship with his high school sweetheart, Terethia Ogden. They met on the first day of school, where they shared a couple of classes, and the senator had started to court her right off the bat. He'd help her with her homework after class. He'd do sweet things like treat her to sandwiches and soda pop for lunch. During classes he would paste one-page notes on the wall outside her classroom door, so when she would come out, the whole class would see his love letters to her. Sometimes he would leave roses taped to the wall with her name written under them. It was beautiful, maybe a little too beautiful. High Schools are filled with young teens longing for attention that they're not getting at home from mommy and daddy. The stuff that Brandon was doing for Terry had the whole school buzzing and most of the girls raging with jealousy.

Before long, the other girls started throwing themselves at Brandon. Judging by the senator's teenage pictures, I can tell he was a smooth operator. He dressed pretty well and had a perfect set of pearly whites and a great smile. Every photo taken of him is dominated by teeth and dimples. He knew he was handsome. To make matters worse, the senator was on the polo and the rugby teams. His popularity meter was through the roof.

Naturally, the girls started to become a problem for Terethia. She began to notice the cheerleaders' skirts were a little too short and their celebratory kicks were a little too high while Brandon was around. The other classmates were suddenly offering their services to do his homework or buy him lunch. They were all over Brandon. As much as Terethia tried to hold onto Brandon for herself, there was always another girl around claiming to just be a friend.

He tells me they would fight all the time, even in public. On the day they got crowned as king and queen of the school prom, they fought right outside the gymnasium because someone kissed him in a drunken episode after having some spiked punch. It was a mess but not enough of a mess to cause any permanent damage. To me, this sounds like typical youth-in-revolt behavior.

Then the senator drops another bombshell on me. One that finally spins this case in the right direction. During their third year together, Terethia had gotten pregnant. Of course, Brandon, being the politician he is, persuaded Terethia to terminate the pregnancy and get an abortion. He just felt like having a kid at such a young age would ruin his future and his playboy lifestyle. He didn't literally force Terethia to go through with the abortion, but he used psychological games to lead her in that direction. Promises of travel and seeing the world only bolstered Terethia's decision.

They hid the pregnancy from the school and their parents by taking her to some backwoods, illegal wire-using clinic that he learned about from one of his polo team buddies. The procedure almost cost Terethia her life. She really wanted to keep the baby because she was in love with Brandon, but he wouldn't ease up with the mind games until she aborted.

Shortly after her abortion, they grew apart. It wasn't the same anymore, he tells me. She grew distant and cold, filled with a lot of guilt because she was raised Catholic, which condemns abortion. *Abortion is never an option in any religion*, I think to myself. After that final year, they both graduated from high school and never saw each other again.

After hearing the story of the senator and Terethia, who now apparently goes by Terry, I let him know that she just moved up to number-one suspect on my list of persons of interest. The senator is crushed. He can't believe his childhood sweetheart is now the prime suspect in his wife's murder. It is a long shot, but I just need time to piece it all together because there are still quite a few holes. I think another trip to Iowa is imminent, but this time I'm not going to be friendly.

CHAPTER 22

I finally leave the senator's house after a long night and go to the hospital to get the proper care for this bullet wound. While I'd been lamenting with the senator, I had started sweating and getting hot flashes every fifteen minutes. My shoulder was swelling, and the pain from it was causing slight dizziness as well. I didn't feel it at first, but when the wine started to wear off, it hit me hard. It's amazing I even make it to the emergency room on my own.

Sitting in the recovery room, I have time to think about the case. Could Terry have been so scorned from her abortion ordeal that she would want to kill the senator? And if so, then why kill his wife?

I get a few more shots and get patched up by the doctor. A few buddies from the Tenth Precinct come by with a few questions about what went down. This is procedure whenever a gunshot victim comes into the ER. When the boys see me sitting in the recovery room with a hole in my shoulder, they want to go out hunting for revenge. They want to employ a little term they picked up from watching one too many gang movies, called who-riding. Which means whoever is out when the police are doing their late-night patrols is in for a lot of pain, especially if that person happens to look like a shady suspect. No matter who it is or where it is, that poor bastard is going to inherit a VPD beat down and a night in the slammer. Most of the victims are drunks and homeless.

One late evening I rode alone with some guys from the Tenth Precinct on a hunt for a meth-head crew that did a smash-and-grab job at a mini-mall off the I-95 strip. They grabbed a bunch of cell phones, iPads, jewelry, and things like that. Tracking the idiots down was simple. We had the owner turn on a few of the GPS police tracking systems on the iPads and within ten minutes we knew at least half of the gang's faces and whereabouts. We burst into their so-called hideout and roughed them up something terrible.

But this is different. I don't need any who-ride revenge missions, because this is personal. It would also turn my hot case cold again. I am just starting to feel like I am getting somewhere with this Jacqueline Caldwell homicide and the Terry Ogden connection. I throw my cop buddies the Richard Lauson theory and how he may have found out where I lived and took a few shots at me. They believe me, but they're still skeptical. I thank them and suggest they triple up on the manhunt for this Richard guy. This will keep Richard from hanging around Caroline County if he is still out there. The last thing I need is some bored, gun-happy cowboys digging deep into my case and possibly tipping off the true suspect.

CHAPTER 23

When I get home it is close to five in the morning and the sun is just starting to peek above the clouds. Sandy and Dominic are sound asleep in my bed, and Dominic is holding the stuffed dog I brought him from New York. For a minute I am expecting Maxy to run up and jump on me like he would always do whenever I walked through the door. When the reality of what went down hits me, I flop on my couch and start to cry uncontrollably. It has been such an adrenaline-fueled evening that I haven't even had time to mourn for Maxy. I stuff my head in my pillow on the sofa and cry for at least twenty minutes.

Suddenly, I feel a hand rub my shoulder. When I turn to see who is consoling me, I see that is Dominic handing me the stuffed animal. I grab it then grab him and hug the both of them real tight. I really miss Maxy, and I'm not trying to hide it. I guess with all the noise, I wake Sandy up as well. I hear the bathroom toilet flush followed by her morning voice, still sounding so sweet.

"Are you feeling better?" she asks.

I quickly wipe my tears. It is almost too hard for me to even speak because I know my words are going to come out with a falter and I

159

don't want her to see my pain. "Not really," I say with my head hung low.

Sandy gives me a rundown of the events at the veterinarian hospital and how the doctors tried desperately to save Maxy. She says the whole staff was in tears but it was just too late. I'm sort of glad I wasn't there to witness that. A dog is like a family member, and I don't know what I would've done if I'd watched Maxy die. Sandy sits next to me on the sofa and lightly rubs my shoulder.

"Can I get you something to eat?" she asks. I just shake my head no. "Do you think Richard knows where you live? Should I stay here? Who could have done this to you, Garth?"

I muster up the energy to answer all those questions in one stroke. "That's what I'm going to find out," I calmly say to Sandy.

I can't sleep all that morning. I try lying down on my sofa and shutting my eyes, but all I can see is Maxy's face. Finally, I get up off the couch and call Wax. He is home cooking eggs and grits for his daughter as he always does around seven in the morning. Usually he doesn't like to be disturbed. When he answers I hear the frustration in his voice. "Six thirty in the morning, it better be good," he says.

"Wax, Garth, I need your help. Somebody tried to kill me last night and my dog is dead."

I hear Wax drop a frying pan followed by a lot of rustling. "I'm on my way," he tells me.

"Wait, wait!" I yell to him, knowing he is as serious as pancreatic cancer about coming down here. Wax is a hot head. The Tenth Precinct won't know what hit them if my partner gets here and they have no answers. By the time he finishes ripping the precinct a new one, there will be a call for a congressional hearing on interstate policing.

"I need you to help me from there, New York," I tell him. "Please. Slow down. Now listen." I run through a brief summary of what went down with the shooting, and I give him the number that came from Judge Hastling's logbook, which his assistant, Lisa, e-mailed me. I tell him to get me a trace of the number and follow up to see if there is any connection between New York and a Terethia Ogden. I have to spell it out for him. "T-E-R-E-T-H-I-A O-G-D-E-N. You got that?" I ask.

"Terethia Ogden, yeah. What's going on, Garth?" he says.

I quickly explain the connection from my end. This Terethia, who now goes by the name of Terry Ogden, is the head of the securities and integrities department at the Multi-State Lottery Association in Iowa. I tell Wax that she was also the high school sweetheart of Senator Brandon Caldwell and that she acted as if she never knew him when I brought his name up. To make matters worse, the senator practically forced a teenage Terry to get an illegal abortion that almost killed her while she was in the eleventh grade.

Wax can't believe it. As far as he is concerned, the case is bust wide open. The Lottery commission put a hit on one of its winners as far as he was concerned. Wax and I have done plenty of scorned women-domestic abuse cases before, so it is not so big of a stretch to us that a woman could hold a grudge for over almost thirty years, like we suspect Terry has done.

I tell Wax that while he's getting information on the phone number, I am going to follow up on Terethia. My guess is that, while the senator is a huge pro-choice advocate, Terry, with what she went through, must now be a top enforcer for the anti-abortion side. Just how far she's willing to go is what I need to look into now. I need motive and the ubiquitous *why* piece of the puzzle.

"You gonna be safe out there, G?" Wax asks. "Sure you don't need me?"

"Yeah, I'm fine, Wax. Just Maxy, man, he's gone. He's gone. But thank God, it could've been worst," I say.

"Why do you people always say that when something bad happens?"

"Say what?" I ask Wax.

"You know, thank God? It coulda been worst and all that type of stuff? I mean, your best friend is dead, Garth. They killed your dog and tried to kill you. Why do you feel the need to say 'thank God'?" he spurts out.

"But I'm alive, Wax! When I'm dead, then I'll stop thanking God, cause I won't be able to anymore, but as long as I'm alive, I'm gonna keep giving God thanks. There a problem with that?" I yell back at him, hoping my level of tenacity will shut him up.

He comes back with, "You know what's the next thing that comes out you people's mouth? He's in a better place now."

"Wax, I ain't got time for this shit, just do what I asked, please. Trace the number and get the info back to me as soon as possible. Text me when you got it. Thank you." I slam the phone down just as Sandy walks in after hearing the yelling.

"Who was that?" she asks.

"My old partner, Wax," I tell her.

"Everything all right?"

"He's just so complicated sometimes. I know we've grown apart since I moved down here, but man, it's like we can't relate to each other at all anymore. Maybe it's me," I tell Sandy.

"I'm sure there was a time when you were going through what you were going through with losing your wife that no one could relate to you either. Maybe that's why you left New York," she says.

I think about it for a moment. I just have to accept what is. Wax is his own person and I am mine. I shouldn't expect anything different than him being a good cop. That is the reason I called him in the first place. He will without a doubt get me what I need.

"I have to fly to Iowa again this morning," I tell Sandy.

"So early? Can I get you anything before you leave? Breakfast, a massage?" she says.

"Nah, I'm gonna grab a bite to eat at the airport," I tell her.

Then she comes back with a lightning rod. "A kiss?" she seductively says. This is another tempting moment for me. I am vulnerable after a rough night of being shot and an emotional morning of losing my dog. Could this be the moment I commit adultery and kiss a married woman? This is the test of all tests, and I need to pass it to feel good about myself. I look at Sandy as she stands there in one of my T-shirts.

"Sandy, as I told you before, I just can't. You still have some things that have to be closed out before we can move on," I tell her.

Sandy mutters something under her breath as she walks into the back room and slams the door. I shake my head, thinking how close of a call that was. As I start to ease toward the door, Sandy comes blazing back out of the room. She walks up to me and plants a big, wet kiss on my lips, to my total surprise.

"Sandy, please!" I say as I back up.

"Please nothing, Garth. You don't see that I'm a single woman? Huh? I need a hug, a kiss, something!" she says with tears in her eyes and a hint of desperation in her voice. "I've been through hell the last few weeks and I'm feeling very suicidal. I need to feel loved again, and you are the closest thing in my life right now. Your rejection of my advances poses a threat to me wanting to live, you understand. I'm feeling very unwanted and lost, in the dark. I need to feel loved, and I need it right now," she yells out.

Having Sandy around me like this is a very bad idea, and having her in my house is an ever worse one. She is vulnerable, and I know it. I blame myself. I was always taught not to flirt with the devil or flirt with disaster, and damn it if I wasn't in a sticky situation right now. It's like going bungee jumping or skydiving with faulty equipment and your release snap fails. You just know you shouldn't have done it, but the excitement and the adrenaline rush turned you on. Now it's too late. You just have to wait for the impact.

Adultery is even worse. It's one of the Ten Commandments written by God, and it's a commandment I surely don't want to break. Growing up in Hollis, Queens, as a teen, I was always caught up in the middle of adulterous living, taking my friends' girlfriends with boasts of better cars or better clothes, only to watch somebody else do the same thing to me the next week or month. It hurt like hell, too. I'd spend so much time together going to restaurants and amusement parks. Spend a ton of money on flowers, dishing out for movies and jewelry for special occasions. Then, just like that, some new hotshot comes around the neighborhood and without spending a dime swoops my girlfriend right out from under me. I knew it was God teaching me a lesson because I did the same thing to get her.

I don't want that with Sandy. She's becoming special to me, and if she is mine she is going to stay mine. I have to figure a way out of this without having this woman do something that will haunt me forever. Finally, I gave her a hug, and I mean a great big one. As I hold her tight, I can hear her moan deep down inside. I feel her body pressed against mine like a tight sweater. She squeezes me tight right back with her arms around my neck. The pain in my shoulder is killing me, but I don't let her know.

Finally, she pulls my face back and looks me in the eyes. At this point I know what she is going to do and I don't know how to stop it. I just whisper a "God, forgive me" prayer and close my eyes. Then I hear her voice.

"I'm gonna respect your wishes, Garth, but when my divorce is finalized, this self-righteous stuff is gone. You hear me, gone," she says while rubbing my face and my mouth and my hair.

This is torture. It is temptation with a capital T. I start to melt like butter in Sandy's soft hands. However, I just can't do it. I ease back and shake my head in agreement. It has to be done the right way in order for this to work.

"I promise, when all is done decently and in order, I will not let you down," I tell Sandy.

Still with my face in her hands, she succumbs to my wishes and pushes my face to the side and takes a step back. "I need to ask you something personal," she says, and I nod my head for her to go on. "You told me your wife died on the operating table while she was giving birth?"

"Yes," I say. "November second, nineteen eighty-nine. The worst day of my life," I tell her as I look in the mirror at myself.

"How did you do it?"

"Do what?" I ask.

"Stay so loyal to God and keep this strong faith you have? I mean, he took your wife and kid, for goodness sake. You never remarried. Didn't you have any animosity towards him? Have some sort of hatred towards God for doing that to you? You seem like a good man, and your life was ruined in the blink of an eye. I just don't think you deserved that. Don't you want to know why that happened?"

Sandy is pushing buttons at this point, just as I am so close to being out the front door. She is bringing me back to a time when I had lost faith. I understand her line of questioning, because where I was ten years ago she is now, and she needs answers. I try to give her some.

"You know, it's funny, but for a long time I was very angry with the Lord for what happened. Then I thought the only way I was going to get an answer for this big question of why was to ask God myself. So from that day on I vowed to be as righteous as I could and do everything by the good book. That way when I die and go to heaven, I'll have my chance to find out the why. Because being in hell gets you no answers."

Sandy ponders my reply for a moment. "I never really looked at it from a spiritual side," she says.

"That was my thought process back then," I tell her.

"What is it now?" Sandy asks.

"Now I have no questions. I just want to make it out of this hell hole called America in one piece, knowing that I tried my best to do it right."

A tear rolls down one of Sandy's cheeks. "You are one amazing individual, Garth. God bless you on your travels," she says. Then walks away.

CHAPTER 24

I fly back to the politics-crazed state of Iowa and head to the Multi-state Lottery Association to set up an undercover tail with Terry Ogden as my target. Last time we spoke she steered me in all sorts of directions with this mysterious murder of Jacqueline Caldwell, but not today. I am focused in on this scorned-woman-with-a-killer-instinct angle.

I sit outside the MUSL building for hours, waiting for Terry to show up for work. There are fast food wrappers from Burger King and McDonalds sprawled across my backseat. I even have an empty water bottle in case I have to urinate.

This case reminds me of that navy captain, Lisa Marie Nowak, who was in some sort of love triangle with another astronaut. The police said she confessed that she drove from Houston, Texas, to Orlando, Florida, nonstop. To avoid making any pit stops it was rumored that she wore diapers. When they finally searched her belongings, she had a kidnapping kit that included a semiautomatic machine gun, duct tape, and pepper spray. The detail that left a lasting impression on me was the diapers. Just how focused can one be when it comes to doing evil? You have all sorts of maniacs pleading insanity across the board after they commit their crimes, but when you study the meticulous methods and details of how the crimes were executed, you see that these people are actually geniuses.

To kill some time while I wait for Terry to show up, I read *The Des Moines Register*. The front page reads: MAYOR APPROVES VETO OF PROPOSITION 8 BAN ACT. America the beautiful is in an ugly state. Though this country is at war overseas in the Middle East, it is also having its own internal conflict with its own citizens. It is the battle of good versus evil, the laws of God versus the laws of man, and it is raging out of control nationwide. In Virginia it is the Partial Birth Abortion Ban Act. In the Midwest they are debating whether same-sex marriages are constitutional or not. Deep in the South and the far West are the wars on marijuana legalization and gun control. Tobacco companies are shooting it out in the courthouses. Occupy Wall Street has spread worldwide and become Occupy the Universe. Egypt, London, Syria, even Africa are all getting involved in the movement.

America, the so-called leader of the free world, is spinning out of control as the time for in-between and neutral is to coming to an end. Now are the days to pick a side and stand by your decision…even if it means death. Some pick a side and Tweet or post on Facebook about it, then backpedal when the heat gets to be too much. Ultimately, they are sacrificed by the media and the public and sent home packing. In a word, what is happening to this country is anarchy, which is the absence of authority or government.

I look at my watch and it is almost eleven o'clock and Terry hasn't arrived for work yet. I am starting to get worried that I missed her while reading the paper. I pull out my phone and call Wax to see if he has anything for me to follow up on. While I am on the phone talking to Wax, he is at his computer doing some tracking. He has a better security clearance from there.

As he is doing the research, I notice a woman in black sunglasses and a black hat coming out the building. Underneath the hat I see blonde hair sticking out. I'm not sure if it is a wig or not. Last time I saw Terry, her hair was black, and in her high school photos with the senator, her hair was red. I don't want to assume that this this woman isn't her just because she's blonde. I decide to follow this mystery woman.

She jumps into a brown Buick Enclave and takes off. I tell Wax to send what he has to my Android device as soon as he gets it. I start tailing the Enclave. The first stop is a storage facility about two miles north of the MUSL building. The blonde goes into a self-storage facility and stays for about ten minutes. She comes back out with a black medium-sized duffel bag. I take a few pictures with my camera just to keep records of her whereabouts.

Next stop is a post office about a mile away from the storage facility. She goes in with the duffel bag in tow and comes back out with a small package.

The next stop is a Dunkin Donuts. She sits in there for about ten minutes, downing an iced coffee and a box of assorted munchkins. Then she hops back in her car and takes me on a winding route on and off ramps and between interstates and highways. For a minute I think my tail is blown and she is taking me on a wild goose chase.

Finally, she takes an exit and makes a left and heads down a busy street. She makes a stop at a building on East Market Street and Jefferson Avenue in downtown Des Moines. While I am driving in behind her I notice the Iowa Civic Center and the public library not too far away. This is a college campus area with quite a few restaurants on the block.

She gets out and walks into a two-story white brick building with blue-tinted reflective glass on the front doors. I sit and wait for a few minutes, thinking this is going to be another one of her drop-offs or pickups.

While I'm waiting, Wax finally sends some information on Terry Ogden to my phone. As I study the information it is clear to me that Terry Ogden is no saint. She has a hell of a rap sheet. And not just a few domestic abuse charges or drunk-driving arrests. Terry Ogden is labeled as a terrorist on the FBI's top fifty list of persons of interest involved in terrorist activity on American soil. It reads like a Timothy McVeigh résumé, listing an assortment of bombings of abortion clinics from Oklahoma to South Carolina. There are numerous accounts of Terry's possible involvement in these heinous crimes, including her being named as a suspect in the gunning down of an abortion doctor named Willis DePaul in Iowa.

I can't help but to think that this is my jackpot case. This is the big time. CNN, MSNBC, HLN, book deals, and movie rights. This woman is a dangerous thorn in America's side. She is clearly on a destructive path and nothing is going to stop her.

I pick up my phone and call Wax. I let him know I am tailing a blonde woman that might possibly be Terry but her appearance is slightly different from when I last saw her. We speak about her being on the FBI watch list and wonder just how far this Terry Ogden woman will go. But I'm still not sure this is her that I'm tailing.

Finally, when Wax asks where I am, I give him the address to the building this blonde woman went into. Wax types it into his computer at home and yells four words that shake me: "Call the bomb squad!"

I look up at the building and realize there are only women coming and going through the doors. Some are jumping in taxis and others are being escorted out. The odd thing about the women leaving this place is that they are all walking very slowly, as if they are in some sort of pain. Then it hits me. This is an abortion clinic.

I yell back to Wax in a panic. "You call the bomb squad, I'm gonna stop her." I quickly hang up my phone and run across the street over to the building Terry went into. I have my gun drawn and, after a moment's thought, I pull out my second piece as well. A .357 Desert Eagle that is sure to stop the drama. I brought both guns with me this time because, to be frank, I am still paranoid after getting shot and I don't want to take any more chances.

Both guns are drawn and cocked as I enter the building. I go to the front desk to ask the receptionist about the whereabouts of the blonde woman with black sunglasses and a black hat.

Suddenly, Terry Ogden comes out of the back staircase from the left side of the building. The first thing I notice is that she does not have the black duffel bag with her anymore. My brain races with thoughts, chief of which is if I'm going to die in a horrible explosion when the bomb goes off. At first glance Terry doesn't notice me standing there with two guns at my side. At second glance our eyes meet. She stops like a deer in headlights and inhales deeply when she realizes who I am. The receptionist slowly crouches and eases her way to the elevators as Terry and I lock eyes.

"Terry Ogden," I calmly say to her.

She gives me a subtle smirk and takes off her sunglasses. Then she looks at her watch, which gives me the impression that I have a few minutes to work with before the bomb goes off.

"Where's the bomb, Terry?" I ask her.

She takes off her hat, then pulls off the blonde wig and throws it on the floor in front of me. "You think you've stopped something?" she says calmly.

"Yes, I do. Now where did you put the bag?" I ask again with a firmer tone.

"Did Brandon tell you what he did to me? Did he tell you how he destroyed my chances of ever giving birth again, huh? Did he?" she yells. "Sending me to that damn butcher shop to kill our child and damn near me in the process. I was just a kid, damn it!"

I'm still not sure how much time I have before this place goes up in smoke. I stay focused on one thing and that is getting to the bomb.

"Terry, the bomb, where the hell is it?" I scream.

She too is focused on a mission and isn't giving it up easy. "Somebody had to stop him. He's out there promoting those pro-choice organizations. Him and that bitch wife of his got all of them up in the government passing laws on who should live and who should die. Who the hell does he think he is, God?" she vents.

"Do you?" I reply.

"You can call me an ambassador of righteous authority. I tried to stop the murder and mutilation of unborn children. I tried to stop the politicians up in their high places, passing their perverted, lascivious laws on the masses. I tried to stop this once beautiful country from turning completely into Sodom and Gomorra. What you have to ask yourself, Detective, is where do you stand?"

I exhale, knowing this dialogue is going nowhere. My most difficult cases to break have been the ones that were religious or politically motivated. Most times the suspects would rather take their cause to the grave then turn around. The fundamentalists, extremists, Zionists, jihadists, and all those right-wing Christian doomsday cults are all part of that internal conflict America is going through. I'm not sure how deep Terry is in with her cause, so I try to reason with her, to let her know I too am on her side with some of the issues she has.

"I'm with you, Terry. I understand your fight, but this is not the way," I tell her.

"I had to do this. Brandon ruined me. Now he's trying to ruin this whole country. Somebody had to take a stand. When I saw that it was his wife that hit the Powerball jackpot, I knew there was nothing that was going to get in his way of reaching the highest office in the country, where he could manipulate our system," she says with conviction.

I can't believe how scorned Terry has become. I am almost sympathize with her and what she went through to drive her to this extreme. That ordeal, thirty years ago, of getting an abortion did more than create a scorned woman, it created a sick monster. But sick or not sick, I am here to uphold the law of God and the law of the land. Commandment number six says thou shall not kill, and Terry is breaking it. I give it one more shot to try to compel Terry to give up before I have to make my move.

"I understand your views," I tell her. You want to rid the Earth of the wickedness and bring back the right, I understand. But this is not the way to go about it. You've made yourself worse than the doctors doing the butchering. You've killed innocent people. That's a commandment you broke, Terry. What makes you any different now?" I ask.

Suddenly, in the distance, I hear emergency service sirens, and there're lots of them. I even hear a chopper hovering overhead. Wax came through and made the call.

I ease closer to Terry because at this point, she hasn't produced a weapon, but I'm not sure if she has a detonator on her person.

"Why did you have to kill his wife? Why not just kill the senator?" I ask her.

"She was a casualty of war, Garth. You can relate to that, right, cop?" she venomously says.

"Where did you put the bomb, Terry? It doesn't have to end this way," I tell her again.

"Yes, it does. Brandon started something, and I'm going to finish it." She pulls out a small black box the size of a pager that looks like a homemade detonator. Suddenly, that overwhelming feeling I get from time to time comes back. My blood pressure rises to the point where I almost black out.

Then, without hesitation, I fire three shots from my .38. Terry Ogden goes airborne, flying to the back of the building lobby. The detonator flies out her hand and slides toward the elevator. Simultaneously, the ATF (Alcohol, Tobacco, and Firearms) and the Des Moines bomb squad come crashing through the glass doors. Followed by two bomb-sniffing dogs and a man in an army-green heavy-duty bomb-resistant Kevlar suit. I quickly throw my guns on the floor and get on my knees and throw my hands in the air.

"My name is Garth Henderson. I'm a private investigator. The bomb is in a black duffel bag possibly on the second floor," I yell out.

As a precaution an ATF agent slaps the cuffs on me and takes me outside behind one of the ATF vehicles, and I couldn't be happier to be out of harm's way. Deep down I am hoping I hadn't killed her. Though it would've been justified, taking a life doesn't sit well with me. This would be the second life I've taken if she dies, and I don't want this on my conscious. I pray for her to live while I am in the back of the ATF vehicle.

After the building is secured and swept clean I see a stretcher come out. When I look, the white blanket is not over Terry's head. She has a few paramedics working on her and some IV tubes attached to her, but she looks alive. I am so relieved.

Suddenly, a cop comes over to me and removes my cuffs. "Garth Henderson?" he asks.

I nod my head.

"Waxton from New York called it in. He told me all about you," the cop says. I smile with relief that this is finally over. Suddenly, I see the cop waving over a paramedic. "This man's been shot, he needs a doctor." the cop tells the paramedic. When I look down at my shoulder, I see that it is bleeding again. Then it hits me. The night Maxy got killed, I still have a bullet in me. All the adrenaline and excitement from this week's activity must've numbed my pain.

I walk over to the ambulance and sit on the edge. Suddenly, I hear a cold voice behind me. It's Terry Ogden. She's alive and still spewing venom from the gurney.

"You've stopped nothing," she says in a dark whisper.

I turn and shake my head in disgust, thinking how even in death the wicked will not repent. "Sure I did. I stopped you," I calmly tell her. I get off the ambulance and slam the door. Knock on the ambulance twice and it drives off.

As I'm standing there, a man with a green Kevlar suit walks by with the black duffel bag and places it in a large steel drum. He nods to me in approval and I nod back. Job well done.

CHAPTER 25

A week goes by, and I am fully rested after spending a few days in the hospital. The doctors removed the other bullet from my shoulder and patched me back up. I buried my dog Maxy right under his doghouse and put a makeshift memorial and wreath over it. I thought about closing the tunnel that led from my basement to the backyard but didn't feel closing off that part of Maxy's life yet.

It is Fourth of July weekend and Senator Brandon Caldwell has invited me over his house for a fundraiser he is having. Believe it or not, the closing of the Caldwell case has given him new motivation to run for the presidency. He says it's something his wife would have wanted him to do.

As I roll over to the senator's house I can smell the aroma of charcoal and barbecue coming from the backyard. The smoke is rising, and the buckets of beer, juice, and water are strategically placed around his huge yard. He has a couple of waitresses and a few cooks to keep everybody fed with chicken wings, beef ribs, and the usual burgers, franks, and fries. Red-white-and-blue banners surround the yard and the back part of the house in a very patriotic display. The senator even has a flag flying high on his flagpole. Scores of Brandon's supporters

183

are here, ranging from politicians to local celebrities and a few big shots with money. Some of the faces look familiar from the newspapers or magazines, but I can't put a name to them. It's a double celebration for Senator Brandon Caldwell as the precursor to his presidential campaign and for the solving of his wife's murder. By looking at him, I can tell he is relieved to be able to just laugh again.

I am taking sips of my beer and relaxing in a lounge chair after downing my third hot dog when I start to play back some of the events that led to this celebratory gathering. Terry Ogden, who did survive my three shots, had just made the FBI's top ten list earlier this month. Top ten meant that at least fifty-five federal agents had been assigned, activated, and were closing in on her whereabouts. With Osama Bin Laden dead, the troops in Iraq back home, and former President George Bush's terror hit list almost complete, the government is now focusing back on homegrown terrorists and drug barons. They have the manpower to do it, and Terry's days had been numbered even before I got to her.

However, something still bothers me. For Terry to have been the killer *and* the head of the securities and integrities department at the Multi-State Lottery Association, she couldn't have possibly acted alone. How would she have had the time to go across state lines, kill, and be back in time for lunch? I had checked her work schedule and her check-in status. She hadn't taken a vacation the whole month. Terry hardy left the building for lunch. I come to the conclusion that someone else killed Maxy and shot at me near my home. Someone else drove to New York City and killed Judges Shumacher and Hastling in broad daylight. And unless Terry is an expert on explosives, someone else made that bomb and sophisticated detonator. I had checked all the vehicles registered to Terethia Ogden, and none came up as a burgundy four-door sedan. Someone is still out there lurking, plotting, and seeking revenge. This case is not over by a long shot.

While pondering these things my phone rings. Simultaneously, the senator comes over and greets me. "I couldn't thank you enough, Garth Henderson," he says while handing me an envelope. It feels like a thick wad of cash. If it's anything over five-dollar bills, I am a very rich man according to my standards. "I feel like a burden has been lifted. Sort of a closing of a chapter in my life. Like I can finally move on," he continues.

"Can you?" I ask while pocketing my earnings. The senator gives me a bewildered stare. Then he backs up a step.

"When we first met, you referred to the killers as them...plural," I say to the senator. He nods in approval. "Terry was only one person, sir. There's been a rash of events that she couldn't possibly have been responsible for, and she has an airtight alibi to prove it. I know you might not want to hear this, sir, but Terry had help. You should alert your security staff of this," I compel him.

He nods and walks away, discomfited. I hate to be the bearer of bad news, but I had to tell him for his own safety. I'm not feeling too safe myself with Terry's partner (or partners) still at large. To make matters worse, Richard is still on the loose after a weeklong manhunt. That is a thorn in my foot that keeps on growing. I feel that as long as Richard and Jacqueline's other killers are still out there, I'll have to keep looking over my shoulder.

The senator comes back over. "I never mentioned this before, but I had two unsettling calls after receiving the tape. A man first, then a woman. Back to back. Threatening calls."

"Were you able to track the numbers?" I ask.

"I tried, but they came from payphones," he tells me.

My phone rings again and it's Wax. This is the second time he's called so it must be important. I excuse myself from the senator and answer. "What's up, Wax?"

He's speaking, but I can hardly hear because of the music from the party. I walk into the kitchen from the backyard.

"Hold on, I can't hear you. Let me get in quieter room," I tell Wax. While walking into the kitchen, I run into some of my buddies from the Tenth Precinct, Detectives Spazolli and Fuller. "Hey, guys, rubbing elbows with the local politicians?" I say to Spazolli.

"Just come by for the food. See you solved the case, huh? Did in two weeks what us dumb country fucks couldn't do in a year? Hell, maybe I'll become a private eye," Spazolli says with a touch of obnoxiousness.

"Nah, just pure luck, guys. You wouldn't like P.I. work anyway, too relaxed for you sugar-rush junkies."

Spazolli walks away with a "fuck you" look on his face. I put the phone back up to my ear.

"You might wanna hear this and stop fucking around, Garth," Wax tells me over the phone. "I finally got the trace on that number you needed from the judge's logbook."

"Thanks," I tell Wax. "Don't think I'll be needing it anymore. We got her. Luckily the bomb squad made it in time, Wax. She was about to blow up the whole clinic with me inside."

Wax tells me to take the number anyway. While I'm writing the number down and looking out the window into the senator's backyard, I notice that Detective Spazolli and Detective Fuller aren't eating anything. With the aroma of beef in the air, you can't help but to grab something. The food is the reason they both said they were there in the first place. Then I hear Wax mumbling something over the phone. I ask him to repeat what he just said.

"I said the number was traced to the police station in Caroline County, Virginia, the Tenth Precinct. Probably someone doing a follow-up being that the Tenth was handling it, right?" he asks.

I don't answer because I can't quite make sense of what he just told me. "Keep on," I tell him.

"A Detective Pilano Spazolli works at the Tenth, right?"

"Yes," I say while keeping my eye on the two detectives.

"Homicide?" he continues.

"Yeah, Wax, go ahead."

"Garth, this guy owns a burgundy Chevrolet."

I look at Spazolli and Fuller. Then I see the senator cross my line of sight and head toward the front of the house. I see Detective Spazolli and Detective Fuller follow him out.

"Garth, you listening?" I hear Wax say over the phone.

"Uh-huh" I absentmindedly say.

"Well, you're not gonna believe this, G. Panoli Spazolli's last name is from his mother, it's her maiden name, not from his father. But guess what his father's last name is…Ogden. Panoli and Terry are brother and sister, G. Panoli kept his mother's last name and Terry kept her father's after their parents divorced in the midnineties."

"You are a top detective, Wax. Call you back." I quickly hang up and follow the senator and the two detectives to the front of the house. As I enter the front yard and look around, I see no one. I look down the street and spot the senator talking to Spazolli. I pull out my sidearm and start to jog down the street toward them.

Spazolli spots me and immediately draws his sidearm. As usual, I'm outgunned. Spazolli has a fifteen-shot Glock 17, and me, I just have my trusty .38. I haven't made it ten steps before I hear four shots behind me. It's Detective Fuller. Damn it, he's in on it too, and judging by his grouping of rounds, he's taking it real serious.

I quickly jump onto an adjacent lawn to avoid getting hit and roll on my back. I get into the firing position with both hands steady, and I aim. Just as Fuller comes from behind a car with his hands raised, I fire two shots. One hits him in the neck and the other in the solar plexus. He's down without a doubt.

I roll back over and see Spazolli rushing the senator over to an idling Lincoln Town Car. The senator fights back. He punches the detective in the face and follows this with a solid groin kick. The kind of kick a junior high kid gives when in a schoolyard fight. It works, as I see Spazolli buckle.

I catch up to the two and Spazolli puts the senator in a headlock and hides behind him. He has the gun aimed under the senator's chin.

"Don't step any closer!" Spazolli orders me. "You thought it was going to end that easy?" he says while popping the senator upside his head with the gun. "You know my sister is paralyzed thanks to you, fucker? And this bastard almost killed her when she was just a child." He hits the senator with his gun again. The senator winces in pain.

"What about the lives you took?" I say while slowly creeping closer for a better headshot.

"They were worthless. Just like this piece of shit." He hits the senator again, this time causing blood to stream down the side of the senator's face. "Thought you were just gonna make all them millions and push your satanic legislative laws on this country, huh? You and that bitch wife of yours? Well, not anymore! Today you die like those aborted babies."

I plead with Spazolli to put the gun down, just as I did with his sister the week before. "Spazolli, please! This isn't the way to go, man. You're a cop just like me. And I'm against abortions as well, but there's only one judge in town...and that's God."

"Well, looks like God needs some help today," he says. Spazolli puts the gun to the back of the senator's head, and it looks like he's going to squeeze the trigger.

"Nooooo!" I yell. Then it happens again. I go into a blackout and bring up my revolving. While drawing, I see Spazolli dump his whole clip at me. All I see are muzzle flashes and smoke, but I hear no sounds. It's like a mute button has been pushed. Fifteen shots in all come directly at me.

I raise my gun up and get a good, clear line of sight between the senator and Spazolli and fire one shot. It hits Spazolli dead center, and his head explodes like a melon. This is man versus machine, David versus Goliath, and God wins, again. Spazolli gets it right in the forehead and drops like a sack of rocks.

When the smoke clears, I see the senator's private security entourage rushing to the scene and a few neighbors running out their homes. I take a look down at myself, expecting to be bleeding from a few holes, but I am clean. It is like the scene in the movie *Pulp Fiction*, when Sam Jackson says it's divine intervention that not one shot hit him. Even the senator looks at me in awe.

"You all right?" I ask him.

The Senator doesn't utter a word. He's just staring at me like he's seen an angel. Finally, he speaks. "Did you see that?" he says.

"What?" I reply.

"I thought I saw a light on you. You didn't see that?" he says again.

"Probably the sunlight," I reply while still checking myself for gunshots.

The senator shakes his head at my answer. "No, it wasn't, Garth. I saw a light surrounding you."

By now the security has reached us, and a few police cars are on the scene. I drop my .38 and slowly walk away from the crime scene. I hear the senator behind me calling my name, but I don't turn around. Another cop from the Tenth jumps out of his car and glares at me. "We're gonna need your statement, Garth. Spazolli was a good cop."

I give no response. As far as I'm concerned, this case is closed and all of Jacqueline Caldwell's killers have been put down. And though I just killed two bad people, I'm not feeling too good about it.

All my life I've felt like I had an angel watching over me. Fifteen shots came directly my way, and not one touched me. I was right all along: God loves me. This is the second time I've killed, and the feeling is no more pleasant than the first time. Bad dreams, shifted spirits, and many sleepless nights are in store for me. It sticks on you for months like a guilty conscience, even if the dead guy deserved it.

Pilano Spazolli and Terethia Ogden were a pair of twisted siblings who thought they could change the world. Though I feel sorry for what happened in Terry's life to cause these chains of events, I know that actions such as hers will always only make things worse. However, it still never sits well with me to take a life.

I think back to my days in NYPD when I would arrest these war veterans and combat soldiers from Vietnam, Iraq, and Afghanistan who had come home after all that killing in those wars. Most of them were just kids when they entered the armed services, kids who just wanted a way out of their mama's house. Then they were thrown into these hostile situations where they were taught to kill or be killed.

I feel that way today. I need some sort of detox, but I'm not a cop anymore. As a private eye, I'm on my own for mental relief. No psych evaluation, no doctors, no police review board. I have to deal with my problems the best way I know how on my own. I just want to go home.

CHAPTER 26

I drive up my street and past my home just to check things out. It is evening, and I have my lights automatically set to turn on at seven. I'm not sure if Sandy and her son are at my home, but I still want to make sure no one's been there. Most perps like to ambush victims in their home when the lights are out. I even do a second spin around the block to check out-of-place parked vehicles or idling cars. Even though I believe I closed the chapter on Spazolli and Fuller and the remaining Caldwell case killers, there is one more person still lurking: Richard Lauson. I am still paranoid; I can't take any chances.

I call the house, and Sandy picks up. When she answers, she sounds unusually excited to hear from me.

"Hey," I say.

"Hi, when are you coming home?" she asks.

"Soon. Everything all right?" I ask.

Then she utters something that raises my red flag. "Make sure you bring some more dog food for Maxy," she says.

I don't respond at first, hoping Sandy comes back and corrects her mistake, but she doesn't. Something is wrong. "Okay," I finally say. "See you soon." I hang up. Richard has found me and most likely has Sandy at gunpoint.

I pull my car around the corner and jump over my backyard fence. I ease across my grass and climb into Maxy's doghouse. Thank God I didn't seal the tunnel. I crawl through the two--by-two-foot crawl space tunnel until I reach my basement.

The house is dark. I hear Richard upstairs roughly handling his ex-wife and calling her all sorts of profanities. Then I hear him hit her a few times. Sandy lets out a scream and a low moan. I pull out my trusty .38 again for the second time in six hours. And though I've just killed two Virginia police officers and feel real bad about it, there is going to be a third death tonight.

I'm in total badass mode as I creep up my basement steps and peek through the door. From the looks of it, Sandy has been sexually assaulted. Her hands are bound, and her face has taken a pretty good beating. She is wearing just panties and a bra, and there is blood streaming down her legs. Richard has duct tape wrapped around Sandy's neck and also wrapped around the barrel of a shotgun that is pressed against the back of Sandy's head. Sandy is sitting on a chair in the middle of the living room. Richard is clearly jacked up on some kind of drugs. He is sweating profusely. He keeps anxiously looking out of the window, waiting for my car lights to appear.

I start to worry because I can't see Dominic, nor can I hear him. I am hoping Richard hasn't killed his son and is planning on turning this into a murder-suicide. Richard hits Sandy again upside the head.

"You like that? Huh, bitch? You want something done, you gotta do it yourself," he says as he looks out the window again.

I have to end this torture. Sandy deserves better. I walk up the last step and pull out my cell phone. I dial my home number, and Richard grabs Sandy by the neck, gets her out of the chair, and leads her toward the kitchen to answer the phone. This gives me a clear shot when they walk by the basement door. As Sandy walks past where I'm hiding, Richard, with his hand extended and finger on the shotgun's trigger, trails behind her.

"Answer it, bitch, and you better not tip him off!" he angrily says.

As soon as Sandy picks up the phone I make my move. I burst out the basement door directly behind Richard. "Hello, Richard," I calmly say.

Richard turns around in shock and breathes a hissing breath when I put the gun to his forehead and squeeze the trigger. He doesn't even have a chance to twitch his finger. *Boom!* He drops like a sack of rocks just like Spazolli a few hours before. And just like that, this ordeal is over. Sandy quickly grabs a kitchen knife and cuts the tape from around her neck and runs into my arms, burying her head in my neck.

"Are you all right?" I ask.

Sandy shakes her buried head from side to side. I know she's not all right, but I didn't know what else to say. What this man put her through is beyond words. I just walk her away from Richard's limp body and sit her on my couch with her arms still gripped tightly around me.

"Where's Dominic?" I ask while holding my breath, preparing for the worst.

Sandy takes her finger and points to the bedroom. I take a look at the closed bedroom door. I hear a TV, but is Dominic watching it? Is he even alive?

"Is he alive?" I hesitantly ask.

Sandy gives me a thumbs-up. I am truly relieved. This has been a hell of a day fighting evil, but it's ended on a great note, with good guys three, bad guys zero. We win again.

Sandy lifts her head out of my neck and whispers in my ear, "I have a present for you." She gets up and goes into the room with Dominic and comes back out with Dominic in one arm and a small Rottweiler puppy in the other. I crack my first smile in a week. Dominic hands me the puppy.

"Her name is Maxine," he says. Sandy quickly hustles Dominic back in the room, out of sight of a lifeless Richard.

I pet my new puppy and kiss the top of her head. "Maxine," I say. I lift her up just to double-check in hopes of it being a male, but it's not. "No worries, I will love you just the same," I say.

Sandy comes out of the bedroom. "What now?" she asks.

"Gonna get you to the hospital. Get us a room at the Marriott, then get you cleaned up. Gonna have to sell the house, it's defiled."

"I mean with us, Garth?" Sandy says.

I hesitate for a moment, unsure how to answer her. Then I look over at Richard's lifeless body. "Guess you won't be needing a divorce anymore."

Sandy hugs me and puts her head on my shoulder.

"Come on, go get the boy," I tell her. I call in the crime scene to 911 and jump in my car with Sandy and Dominic.

"You saved my life twice," Sandy tells me. "I'm indebted to you forever."

I think of a line that Sam Spade said in *The Maltese Falcon*. "You gotta convince me that you know what this is all about, that you aren't just fiddling around hoping it'll all come out right in the end."

Sandy doesn't even respond. She just cuddles up next to me in the front seat of the car and lays her head on my shoulder. I pull off with my new family in tow. *Guy gets girl.* Welcome to the world according to Garth.

*** THE END ***